TABLE OF CONTENTS

KU-197-200

INTRODUCING...

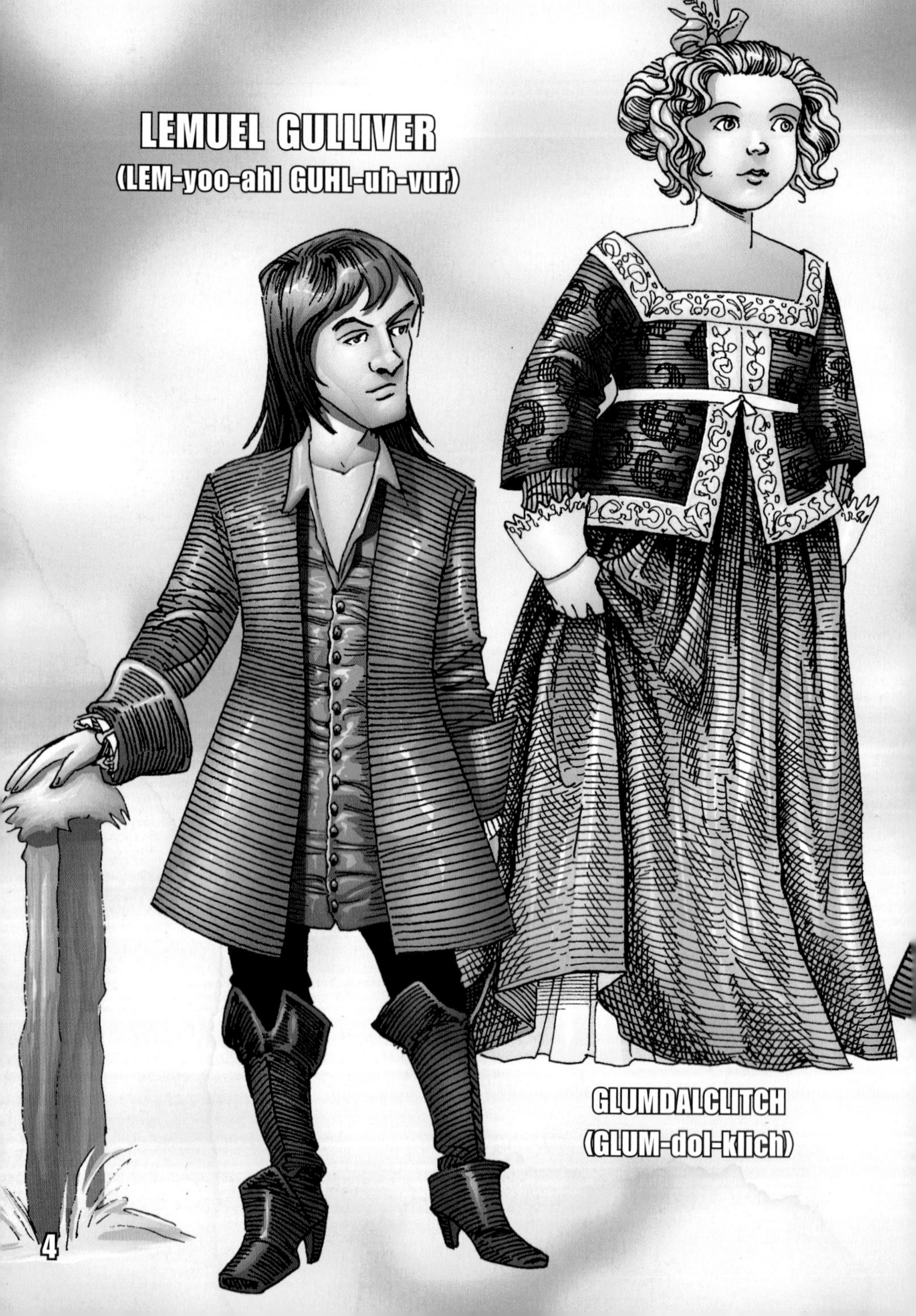
LEMUEL GULLIVER
(LEM-yoo-ahl GUHL-uh-vur)
GLUMDALCLITCH
(GLUM-dol-klich)

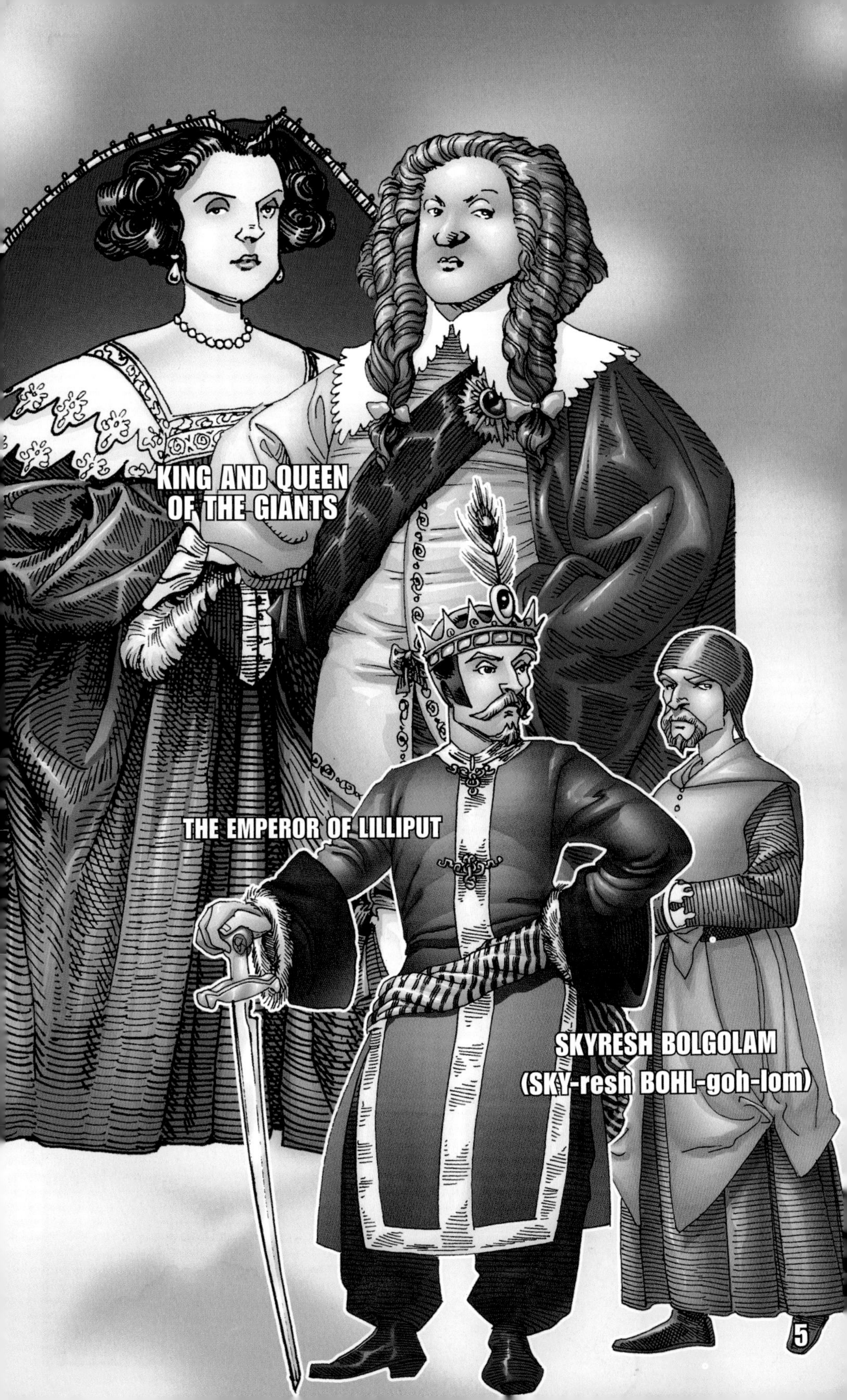
KING AND QUEEN OF THE GIANTS
THE EMPEROR OF LILLIPUT
SKYRESH BOLGOLAM (SKY-resh BOHL-goh-lom)

CHAPTER 1: VOYAGE TO LILLIPUT

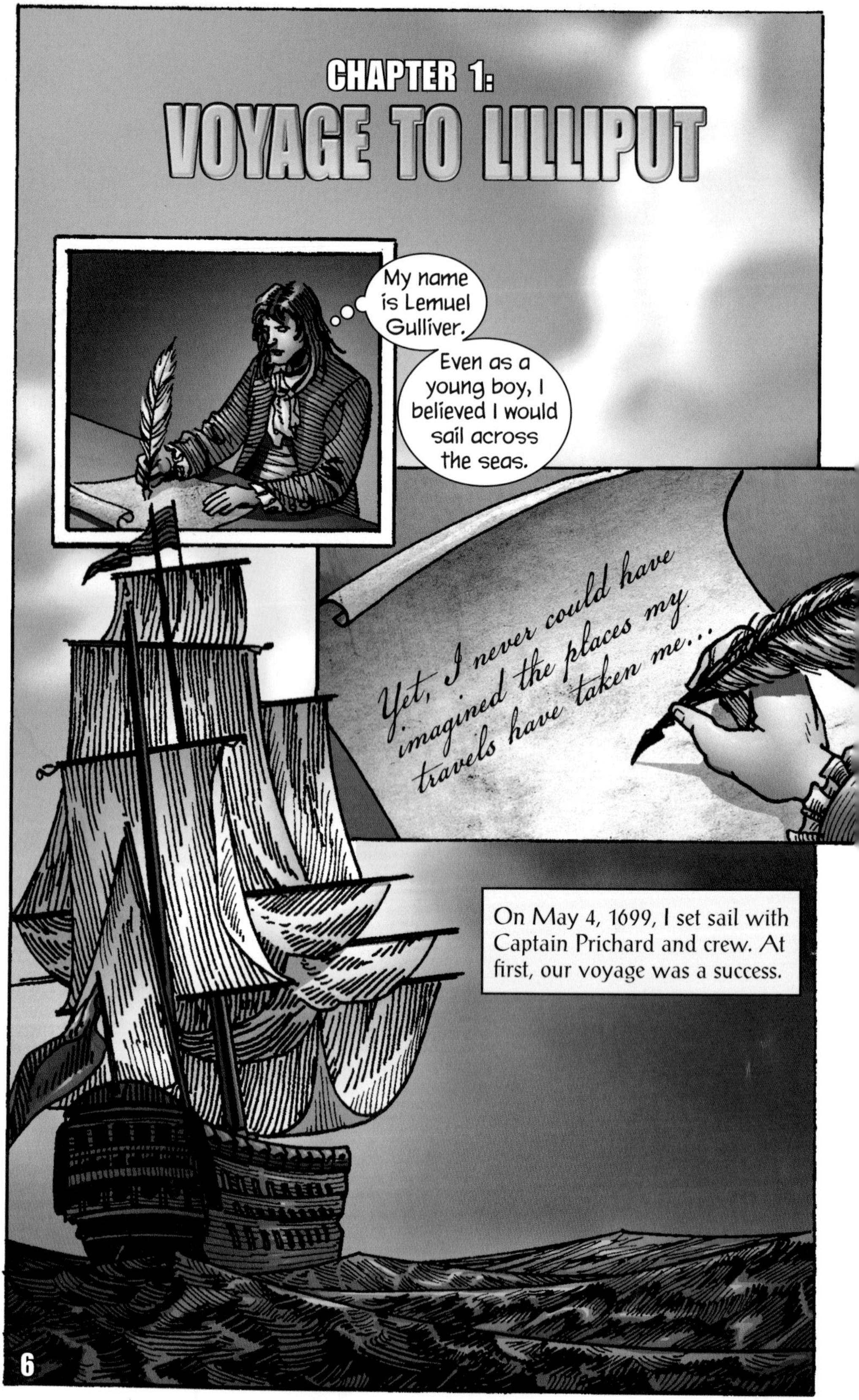
My name is Lemuel Gulliver.
Even as a young boy, I believed I would sail across the seas.
Yet, I never could have imagined the places my travels have taken me...
On May 4, 1699, I set sail with Captain Prichard and crew. At first, our voyage was a success.

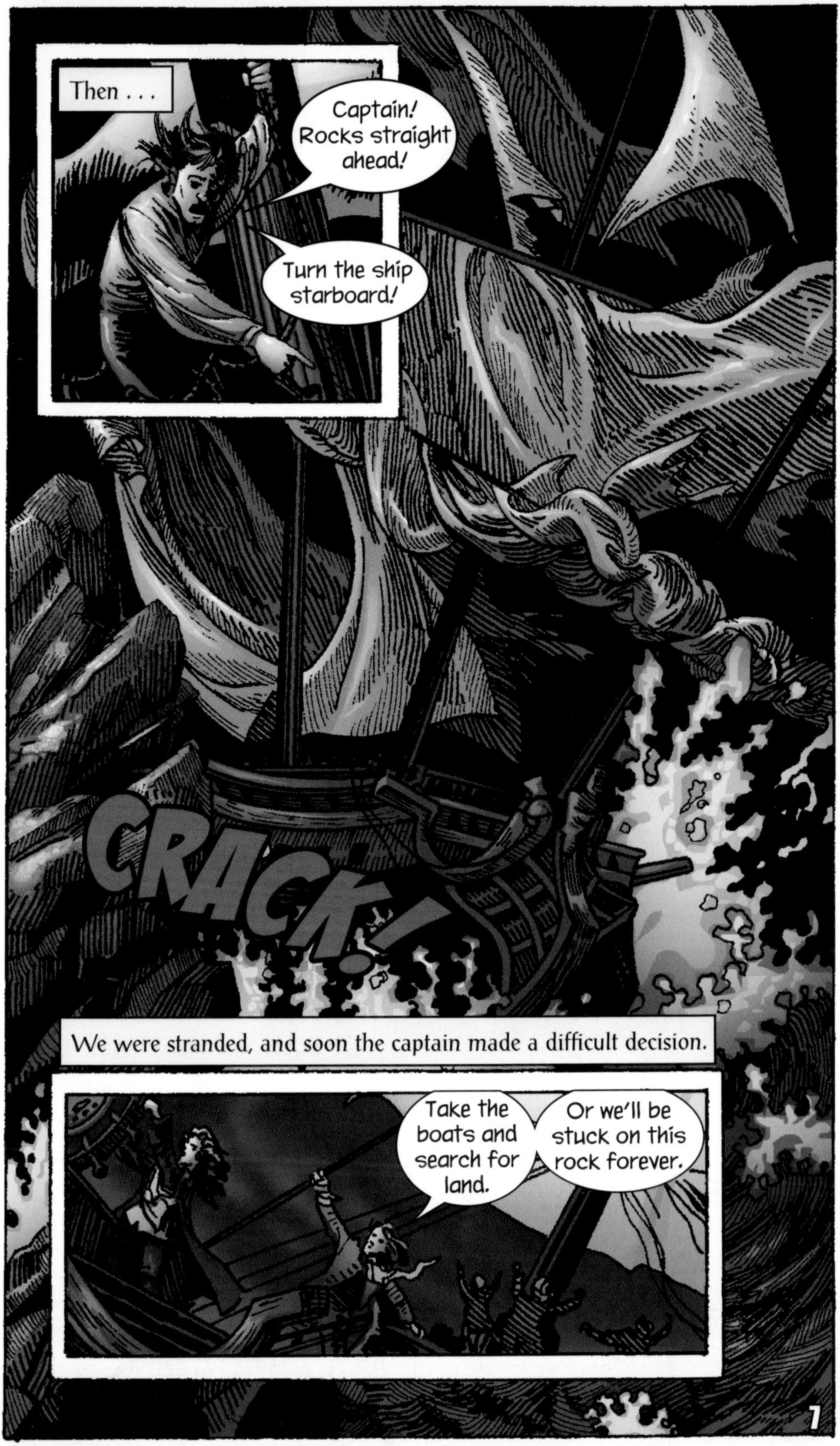
Then . . .
Captain! Rocks straight ahead!
Turn the ship starboard!
CRACK!
We were stranded, and soon the captain made a difficult decision.
Take the boats and search for land.
Or we'll be stuck on this rock forever.

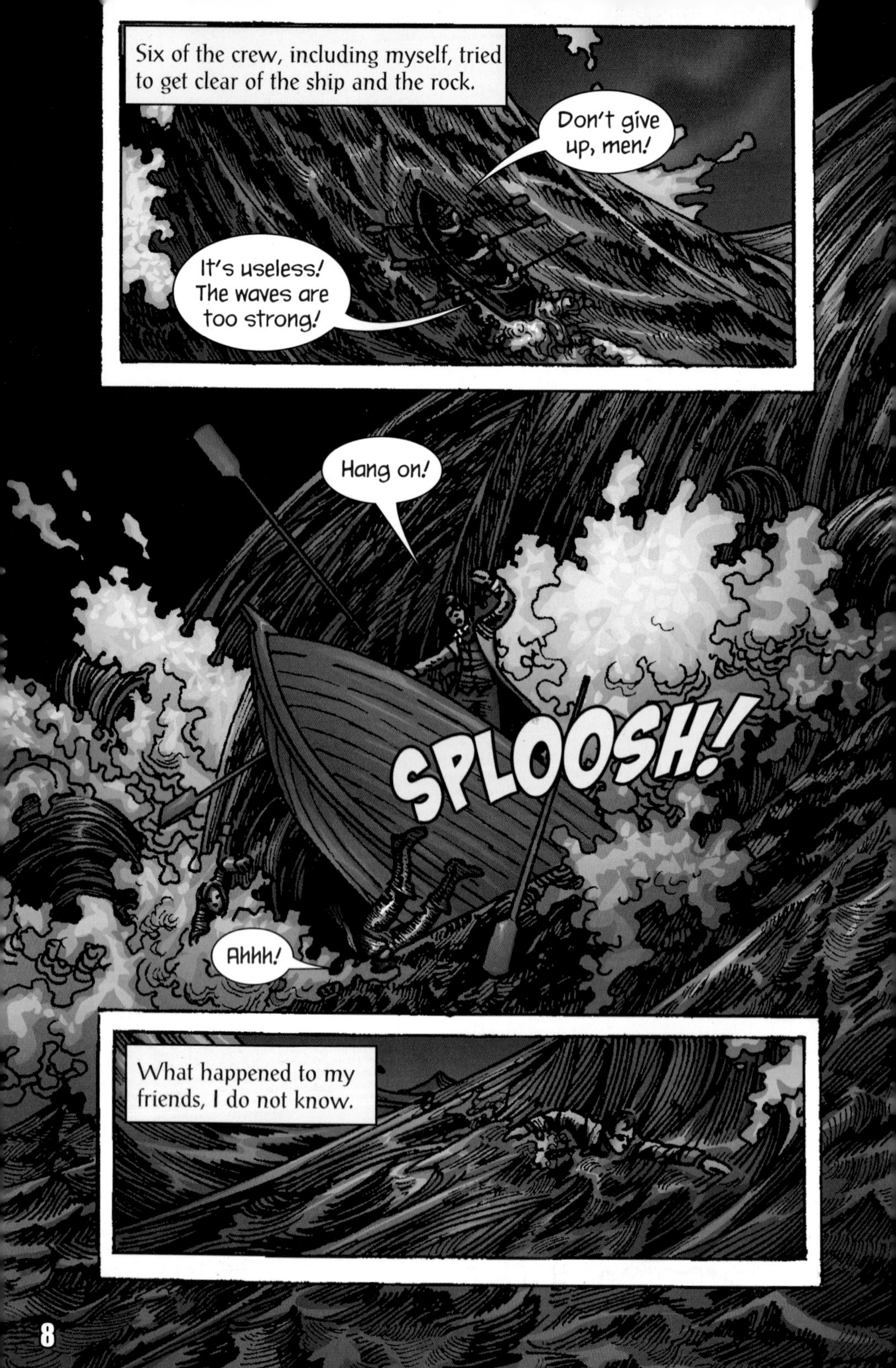
Six of the crew, including myself, tried to get clear of the ship and the rock.
Don't give up, men!
It's useless! The waves are too strong!
Hang on!
SPLOOSH!
Ahhh!
What happened to my friends, I do not know.

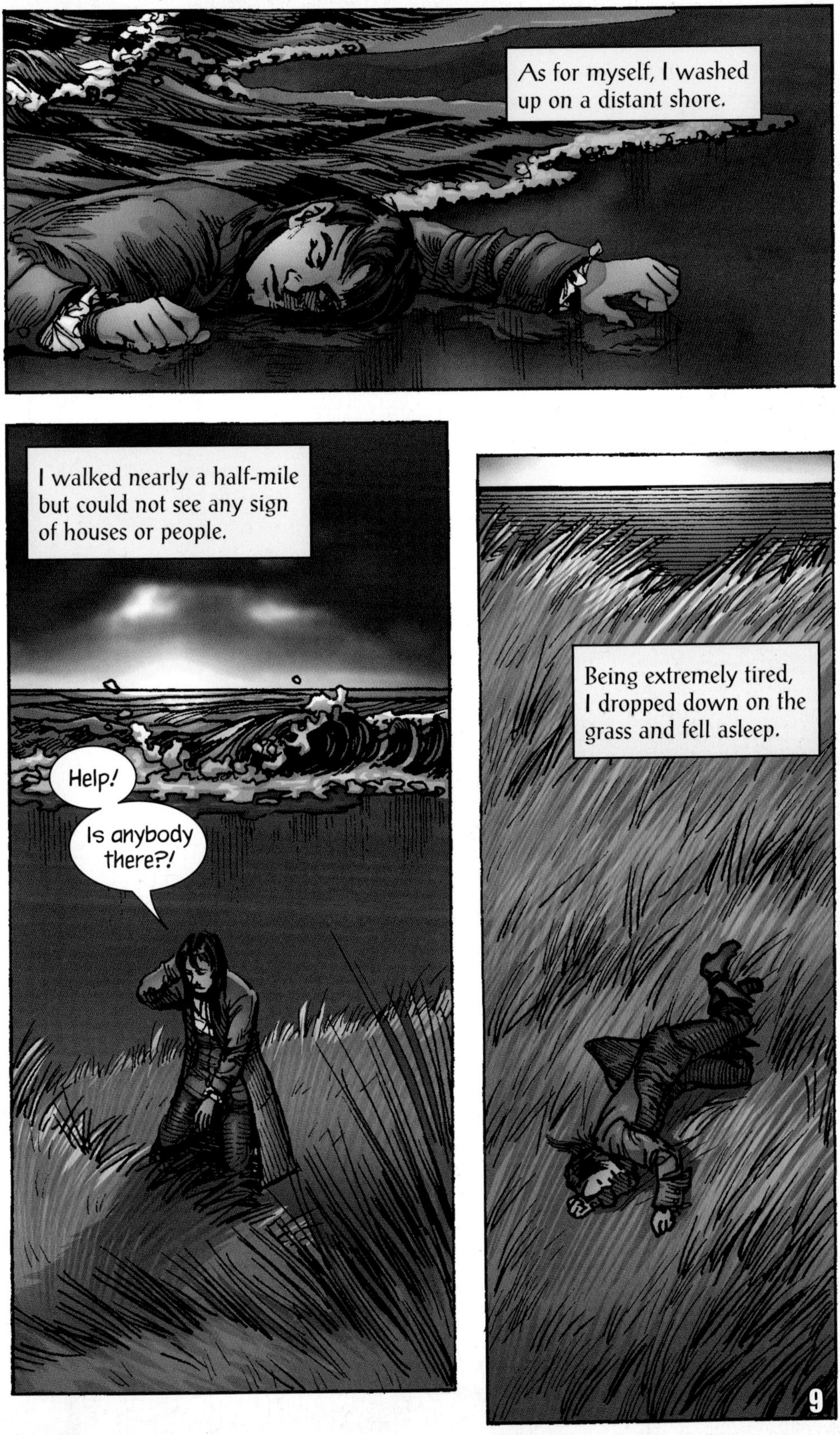
As for myself, I washed up on a distant shore.
I walked nearly a half-mile but could not see any sign of houses or people.
Help!
Is anybody there?!
Being extremely tired, I dropped down on the grass and fell asleep.

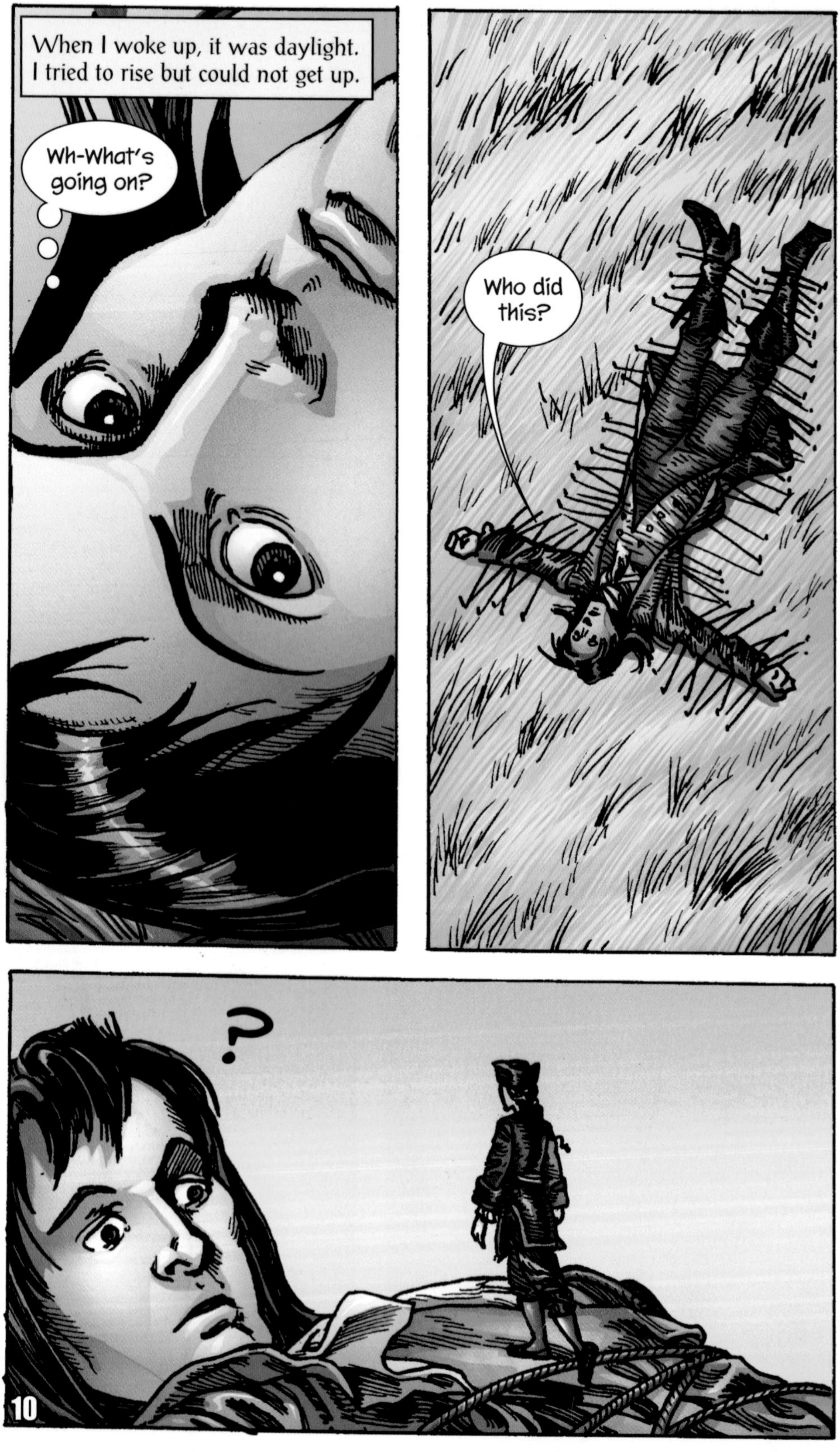
When I woke up, it was daylight. I tried to rise but could not get up.
Wh-What's going on?
Who did this?
?

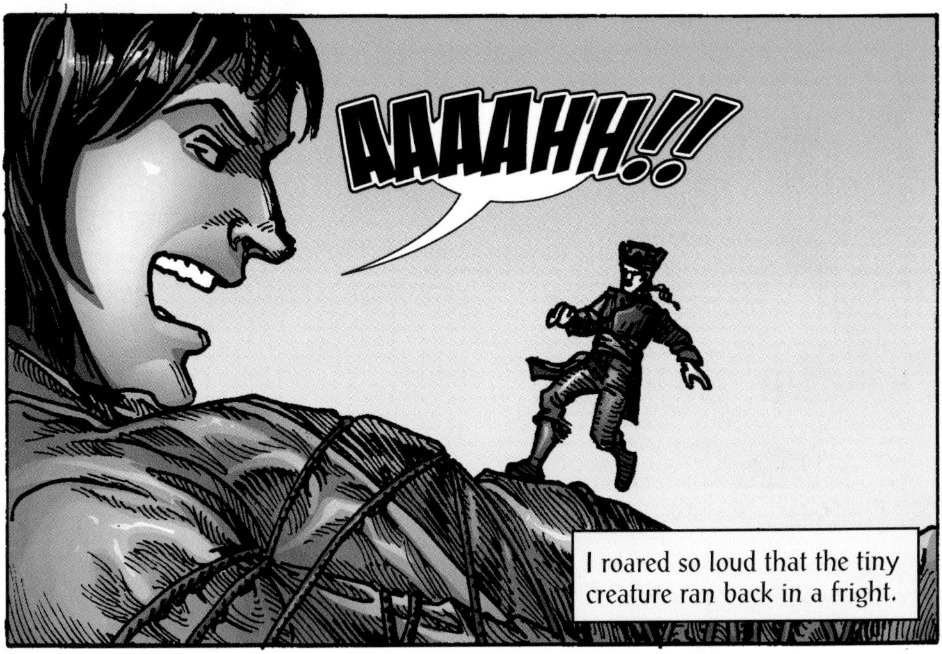
AAAAHH!!
I roared so loud that the tiny creature ran back in a fright.

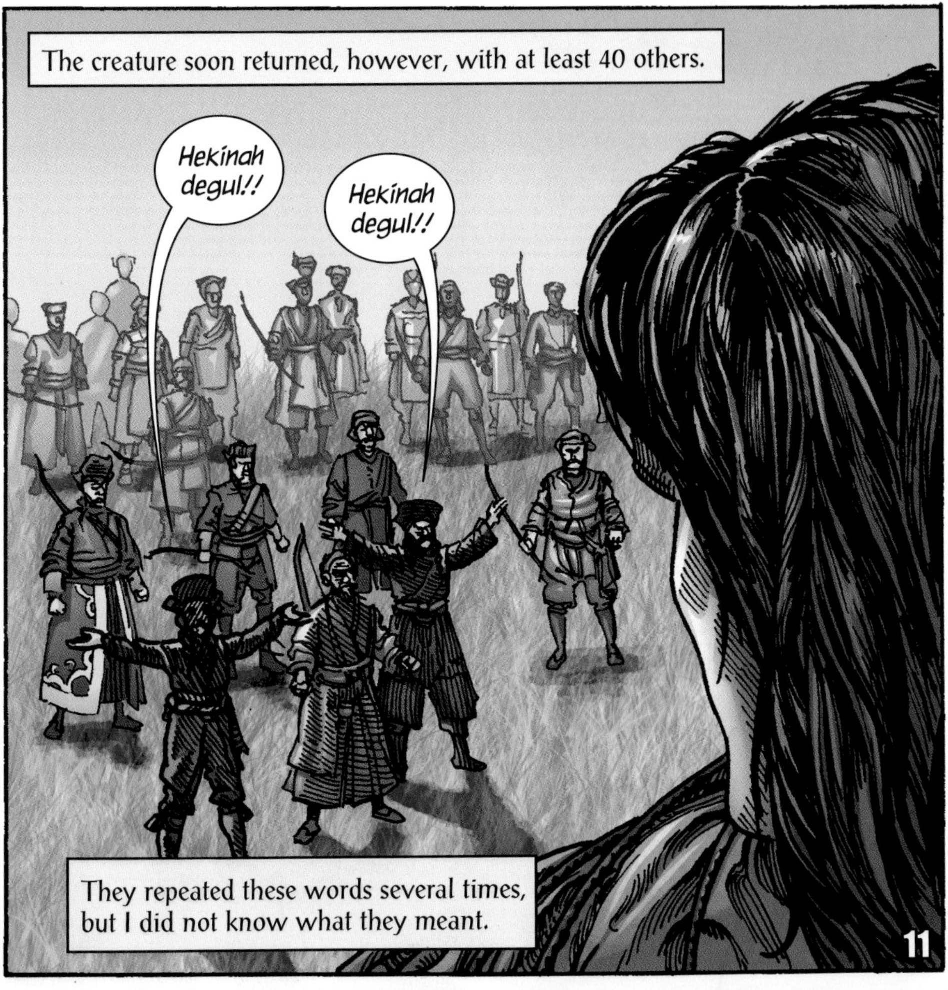
The creature soon returned, however, with at least 40 others.
Hekinah degul!!
Hekinah degul!!
They repeated these words several times, but I did not know what they meant.

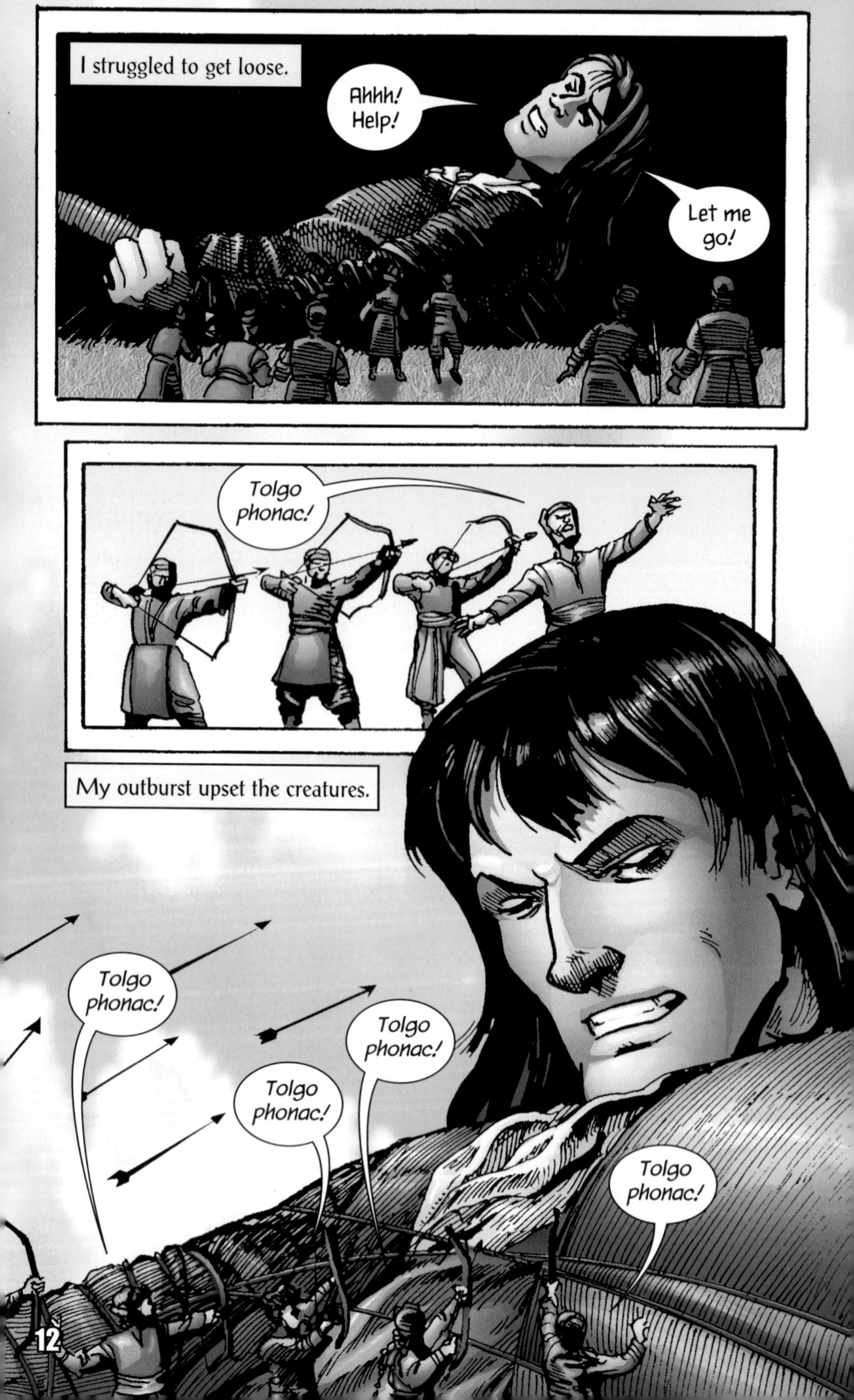
I struggled to get loose.
Ahhh! Help!
Let me go!
Tolgo phonac!
My outburst upset the creatures.
Tolgo phonac!
Tolgo phonac!
Tolgo phonac!
Tolgo phonac!

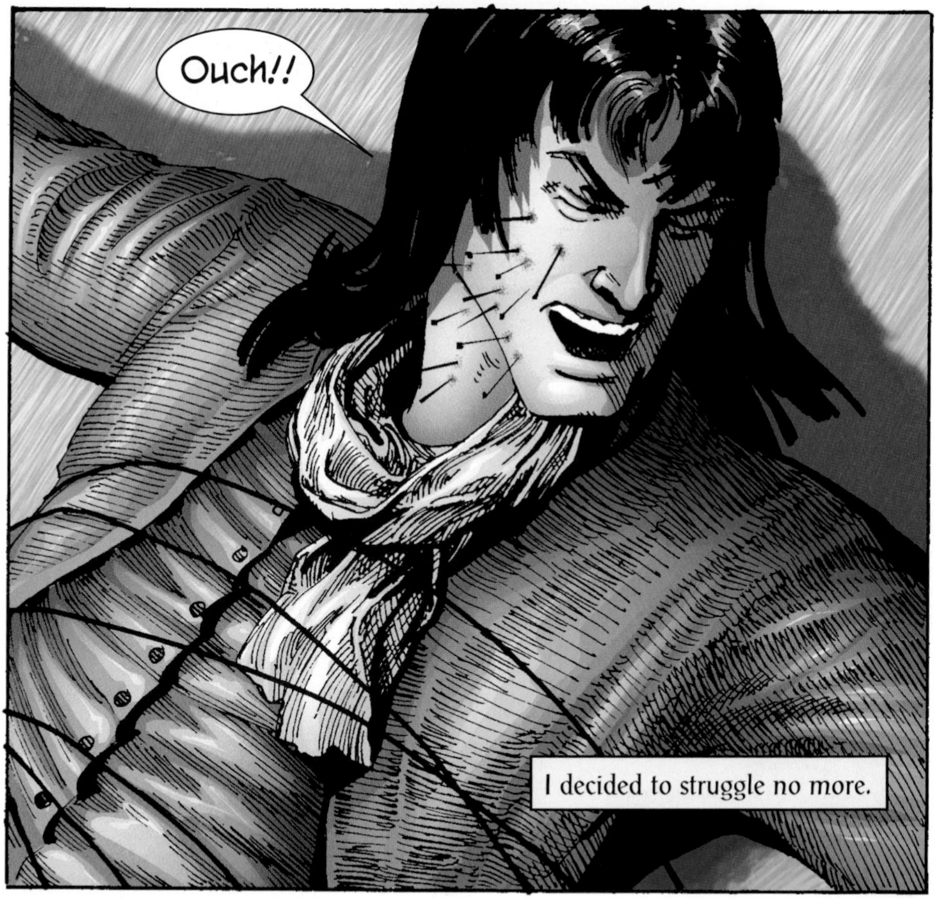
Ouch!!
I decided to struggle no more.

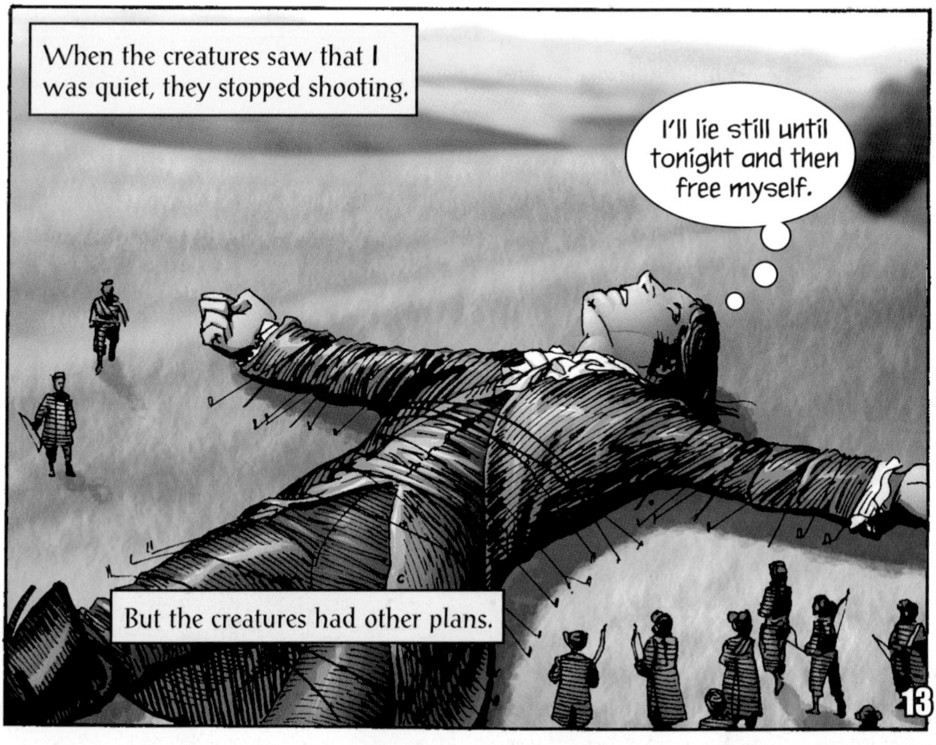
When the creatures saw that I was quiet, they stopped shooting.
I'll lie still until tonight and then free myself.
But the creatures had other plans.

CHAPTER 2: MEETING THE EMPEROR

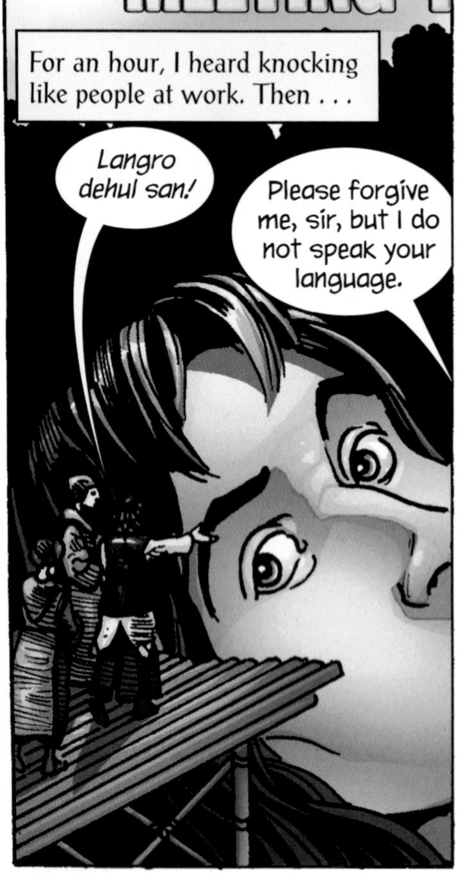
For an hour, I heard knocking like people at work. Then . . .
Langro dehul san!
Please forgive me, sir, but I do not speak your language.

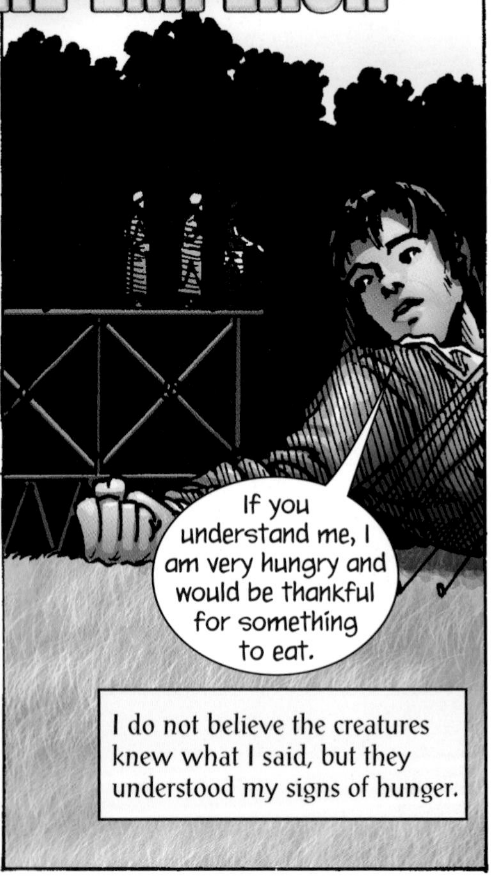
If you understand me, I am very hungry and would be thankful for something to eat.
I do not believe the creatures knew what I said, but they understood my signs of hunger.

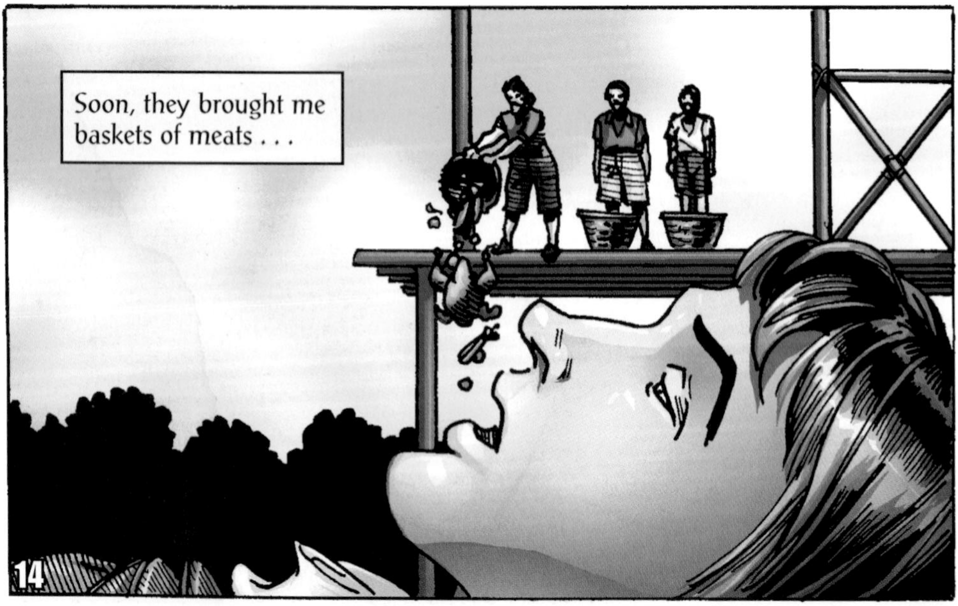
Soon, they brought me baskets of meats . . .

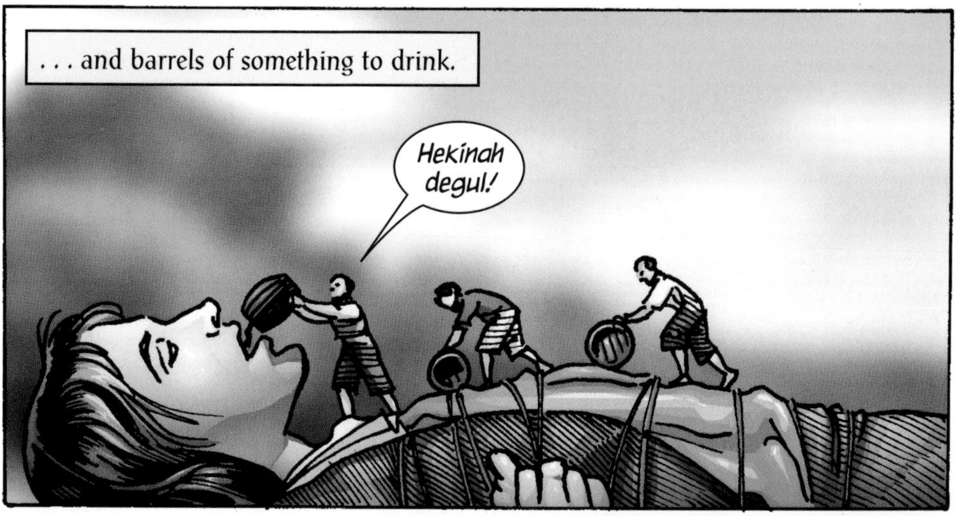
. . . and barrels of something to drink.
Hekinah degul!

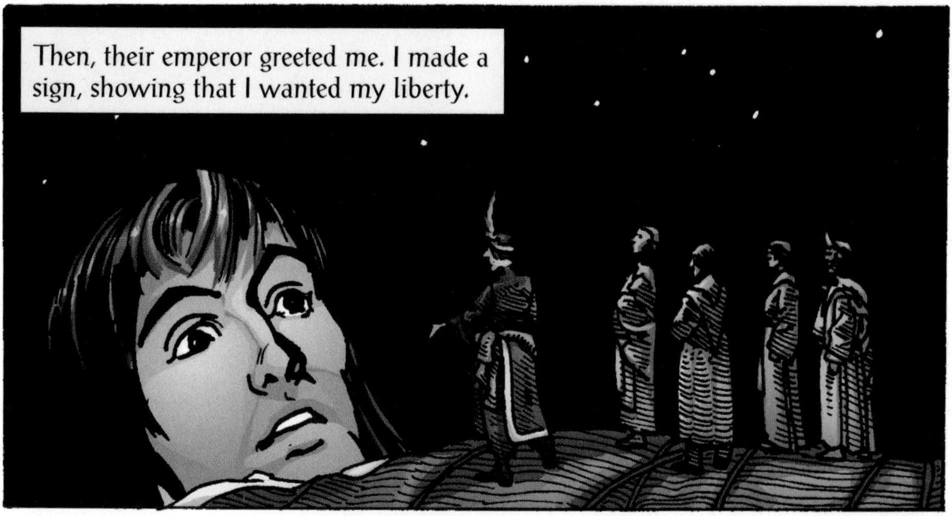
Then, their emperor greeted me. I made a sign, showing that I wanted my liberty.

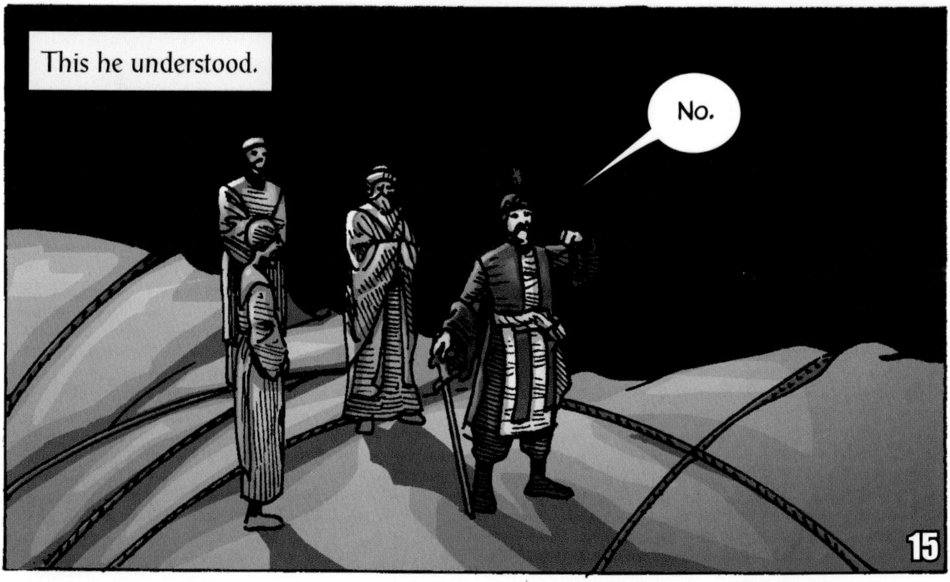
This he understood.
No.

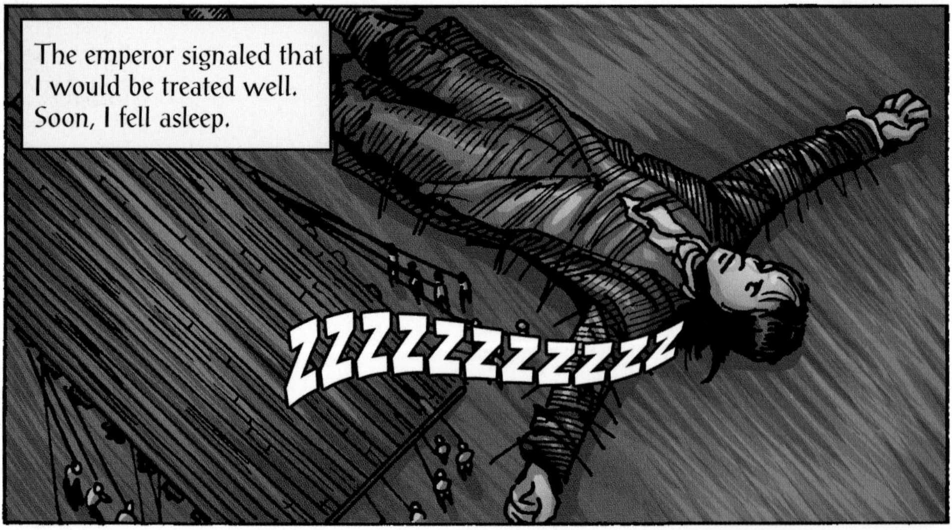
The emperor signaled that I would be treated well. Soon, I fell asleep.
ZZZZZZZZZZZZ

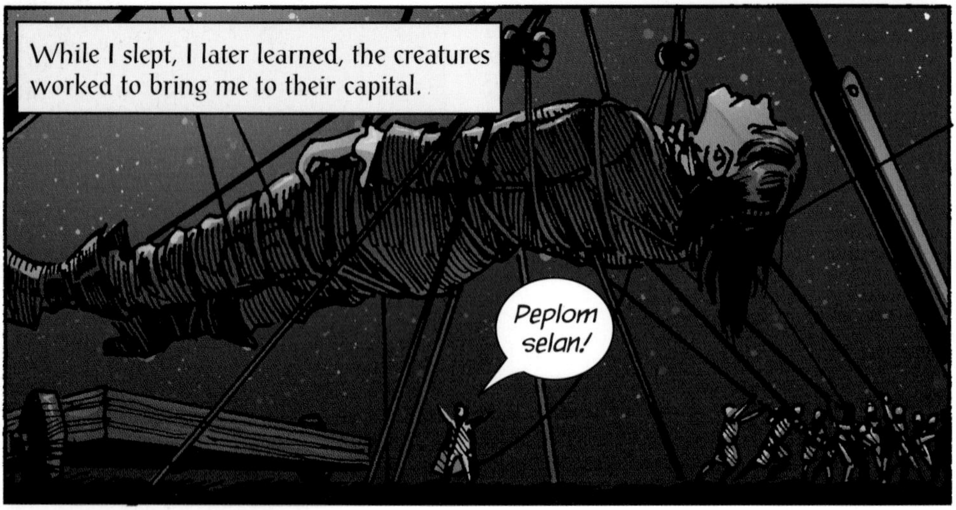
While I slept, I later learned, the creatures worked to bring me to their capital.
Peplom selan!

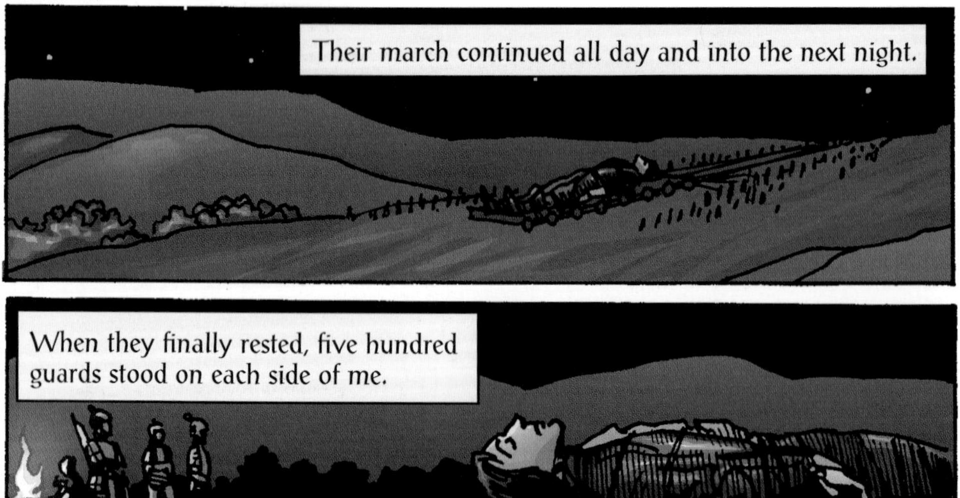
Their march continued all day and into the next night.

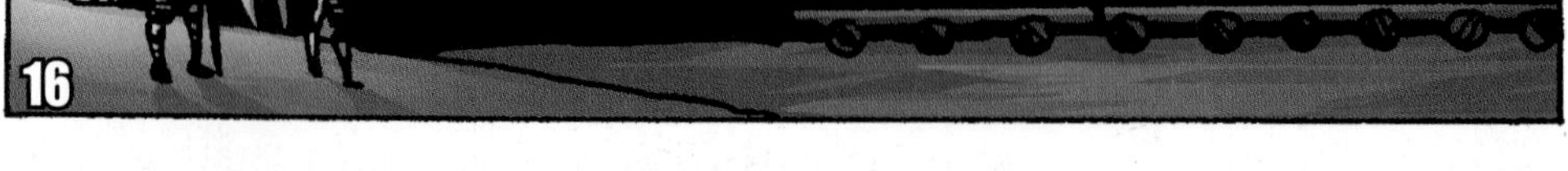
When they finally rested, five hundred guards stood on each side of me.

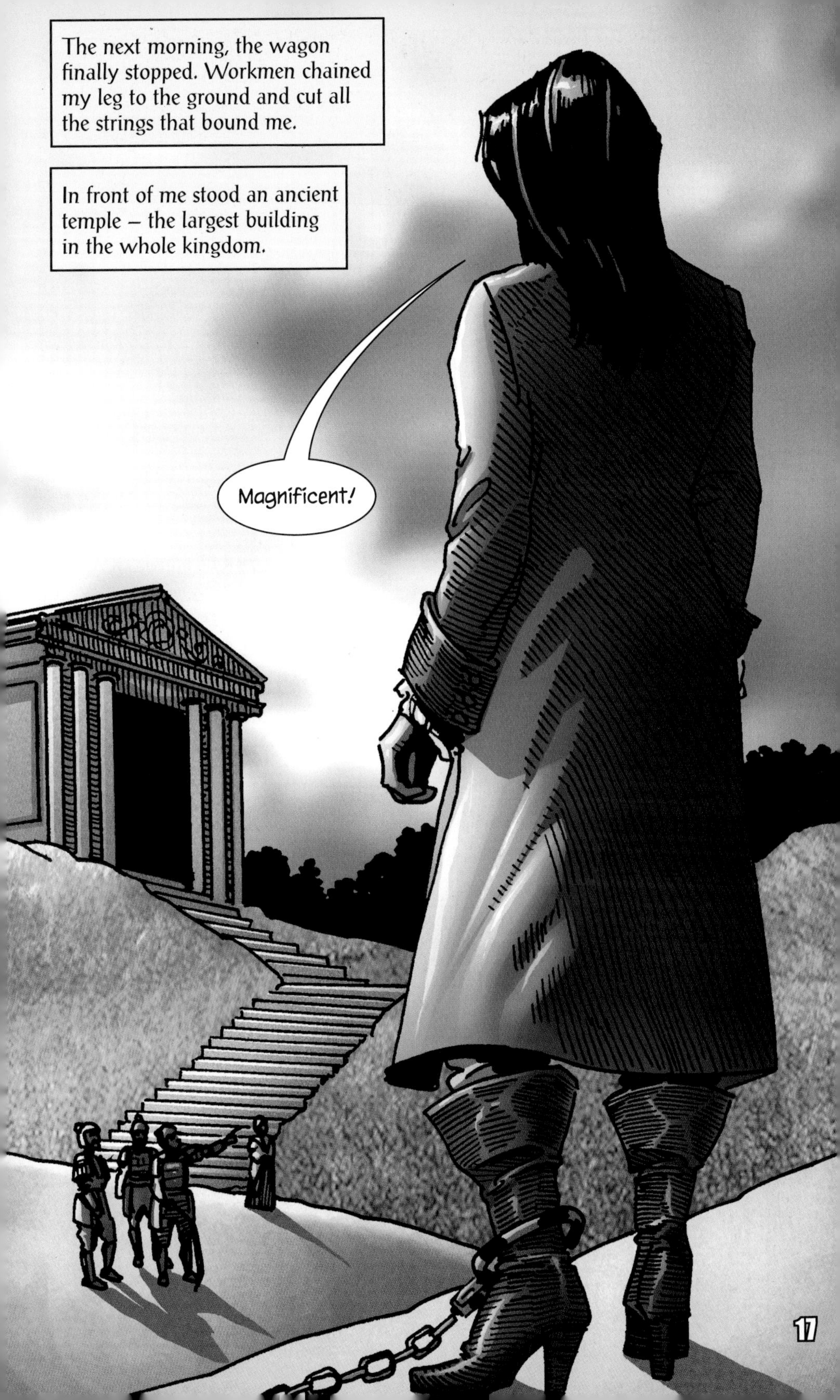
The next morning, the wagon finally stopped. Workmen chained my leg to the ground and cut all the strings that bound me.
In front of me stood an ancient temple – the largest building in the whole kingdom.
Magnificent!

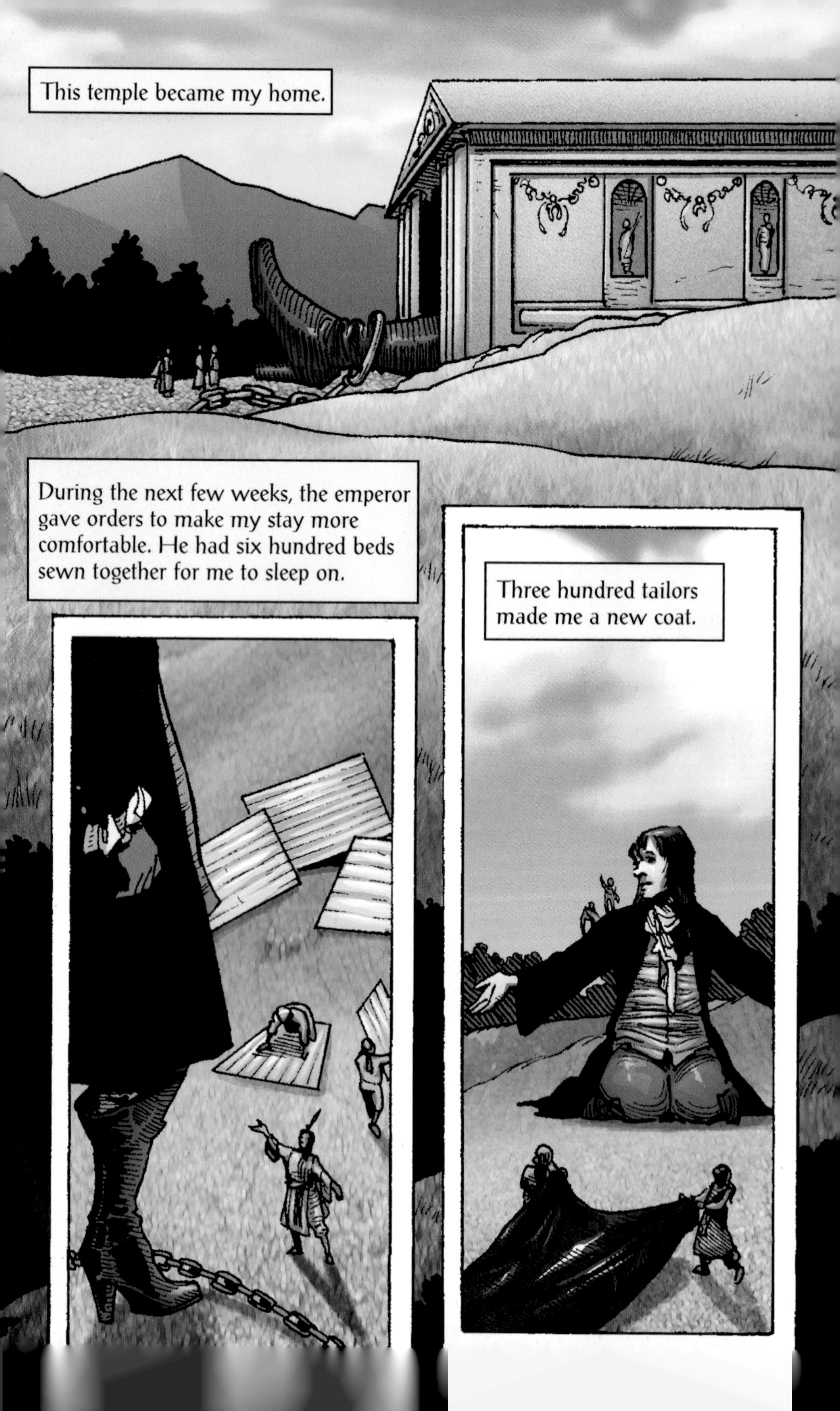
This temple became my home.
During the next few weeks, the emperor gave orders to make my stay more comfortable. He had six hundred beds sewn together for me to sleep on.
Three hundred tailors made me a new coat.

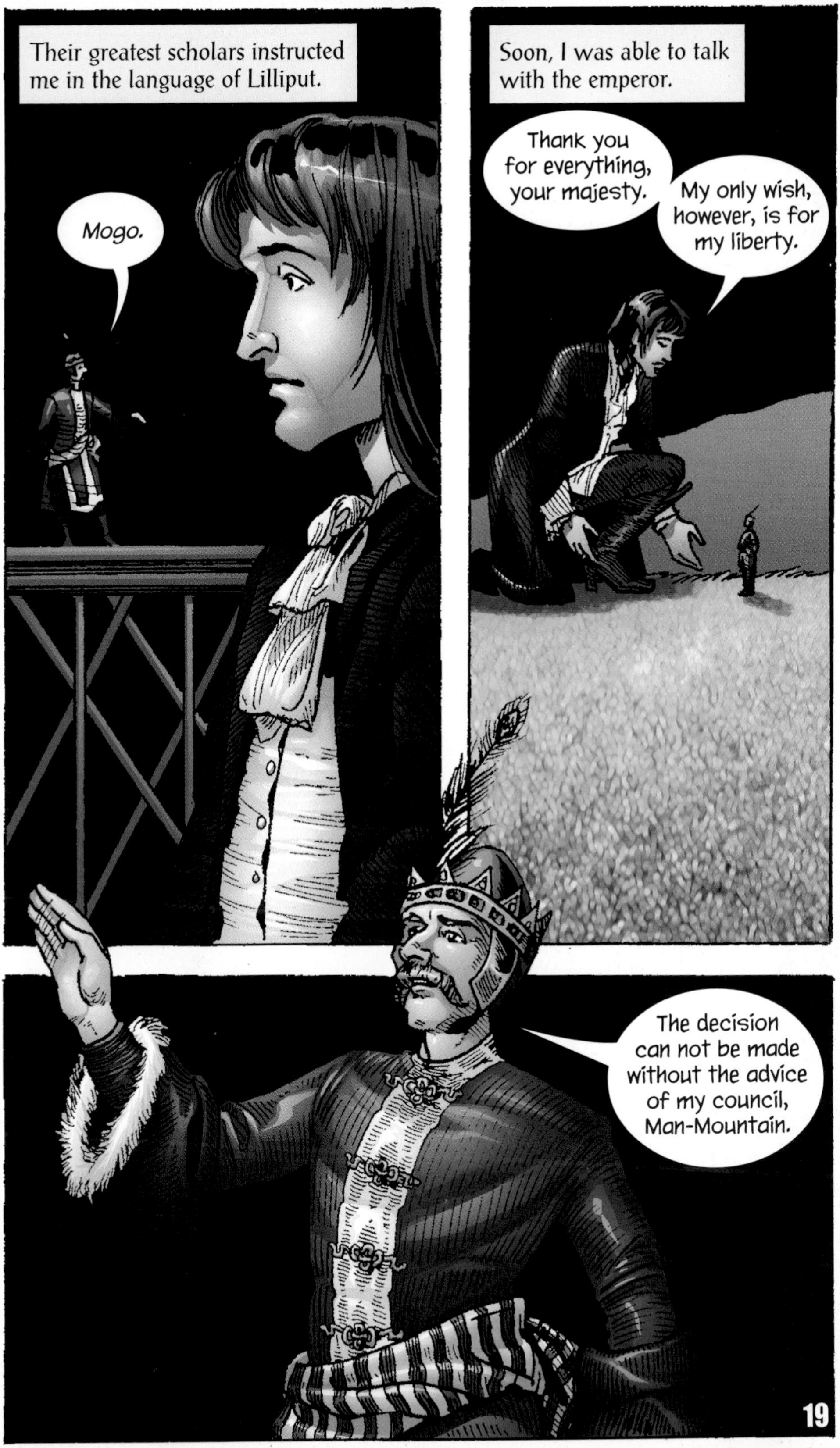

Their greatest scholars instructed me in the language of Lilliput.
Mogo.
Soon, I was able to talk with the emperor.
Thank you for everything, your majesty.
My only wish, however, is for my liberty.
The decision can not be made without the advice of my council, Man-Mountain.

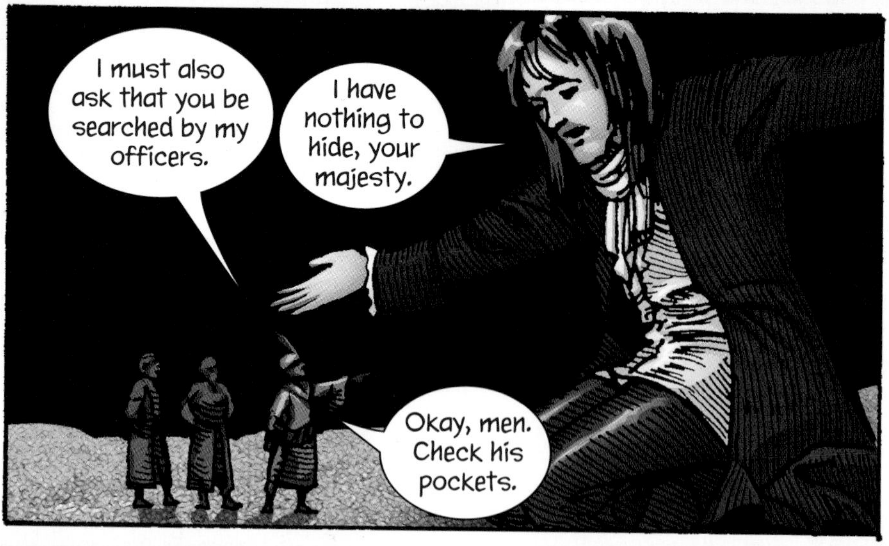
I must also ask that you be searched by my officers.
I have nothing to hide, your majesty.
Okay, men. Check his pockets.

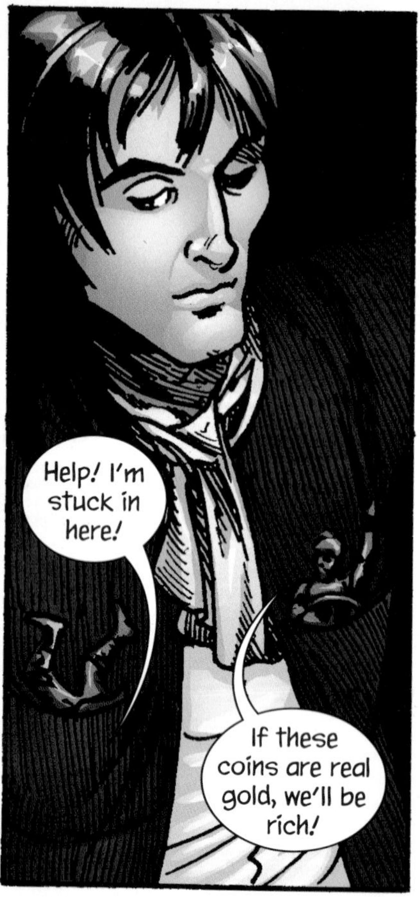
Help! I'm stuck in here!
If these coins are real gold, we'll be rich!

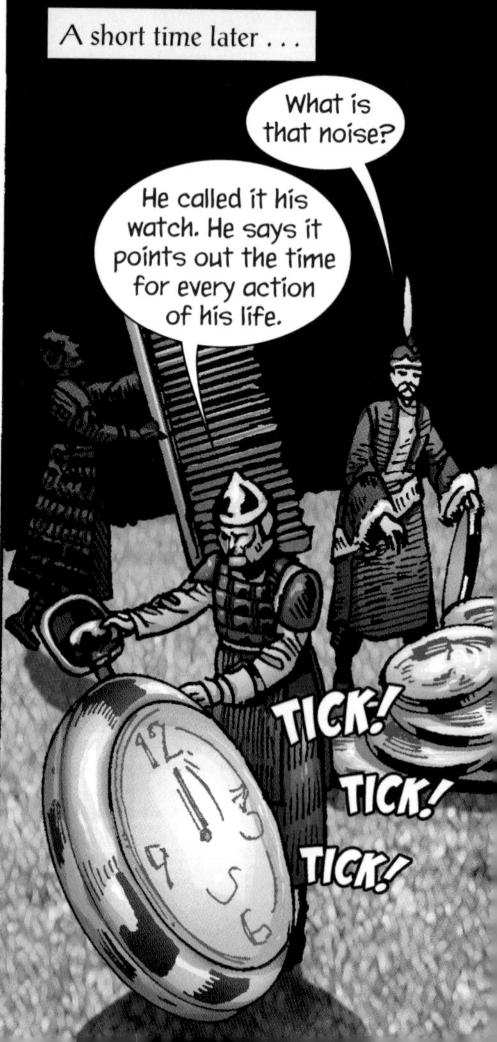
A short time later . . .
What is that noise?
He called it his watch. He says it points out the time for every action of his life.
TICK!
TICK!
TICK!

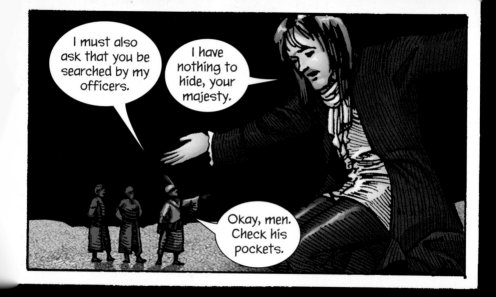

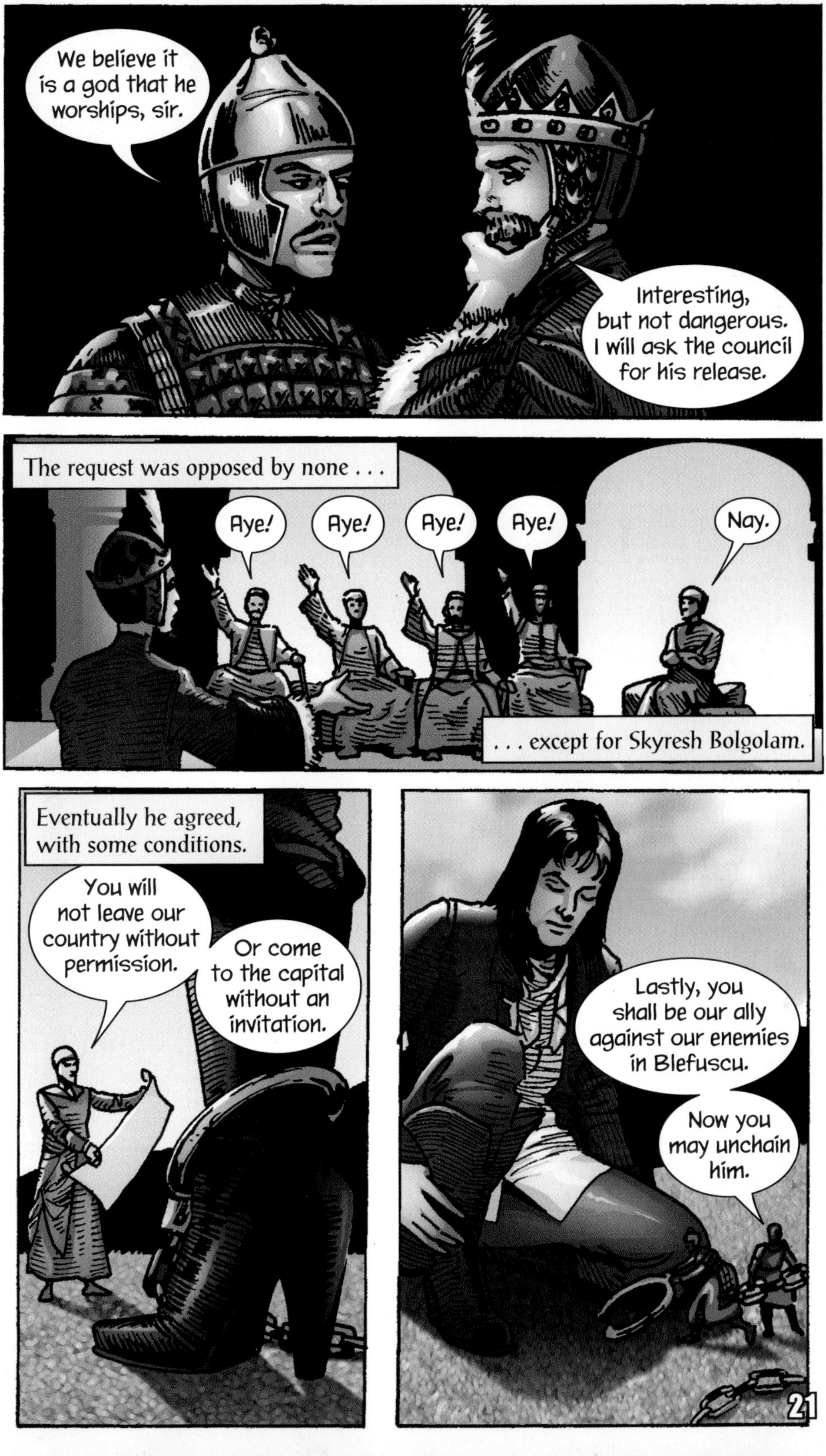

We believe it is a god that he worships, sir.
Interesting, but not dangerous. I will ask the council for his release.
The request was opposed by none . . .
Aye!
Aye!
Aye!
Aye!
Nay.
. . . except for Skyresh Bolgolam.
Eventually he agreed, with some conditions.
You will not leave our country without permission.
Or come to the capital without an invitation.
Lastly, you shall be our ally against our enemies in Blefuscu.
Now you may unchain him.

CHAPTER 3:
THE WAR WITH BLEFUSCU

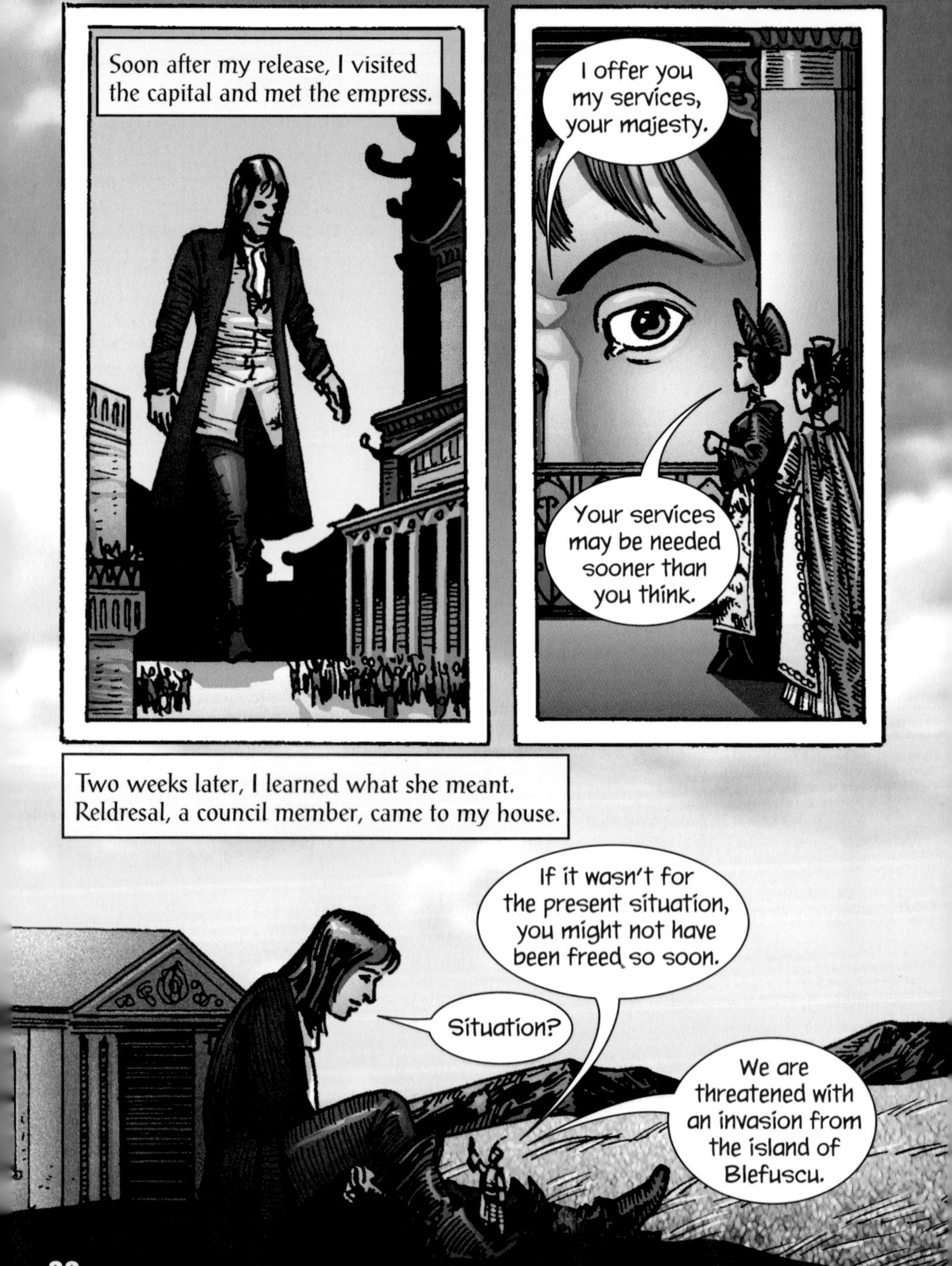
Soon after my release, I visited the capital and met the empress.
I offer you my services, your majesty.
Your services may be needed sooner than you think.
Two weeks later, I learned what she meant. Reldresal, a council member, came to my house.
If it wasn't for the present situation, you might not have been freed so soon.
Situation?
We are threatened with an invasion from the island of Blefuscu.

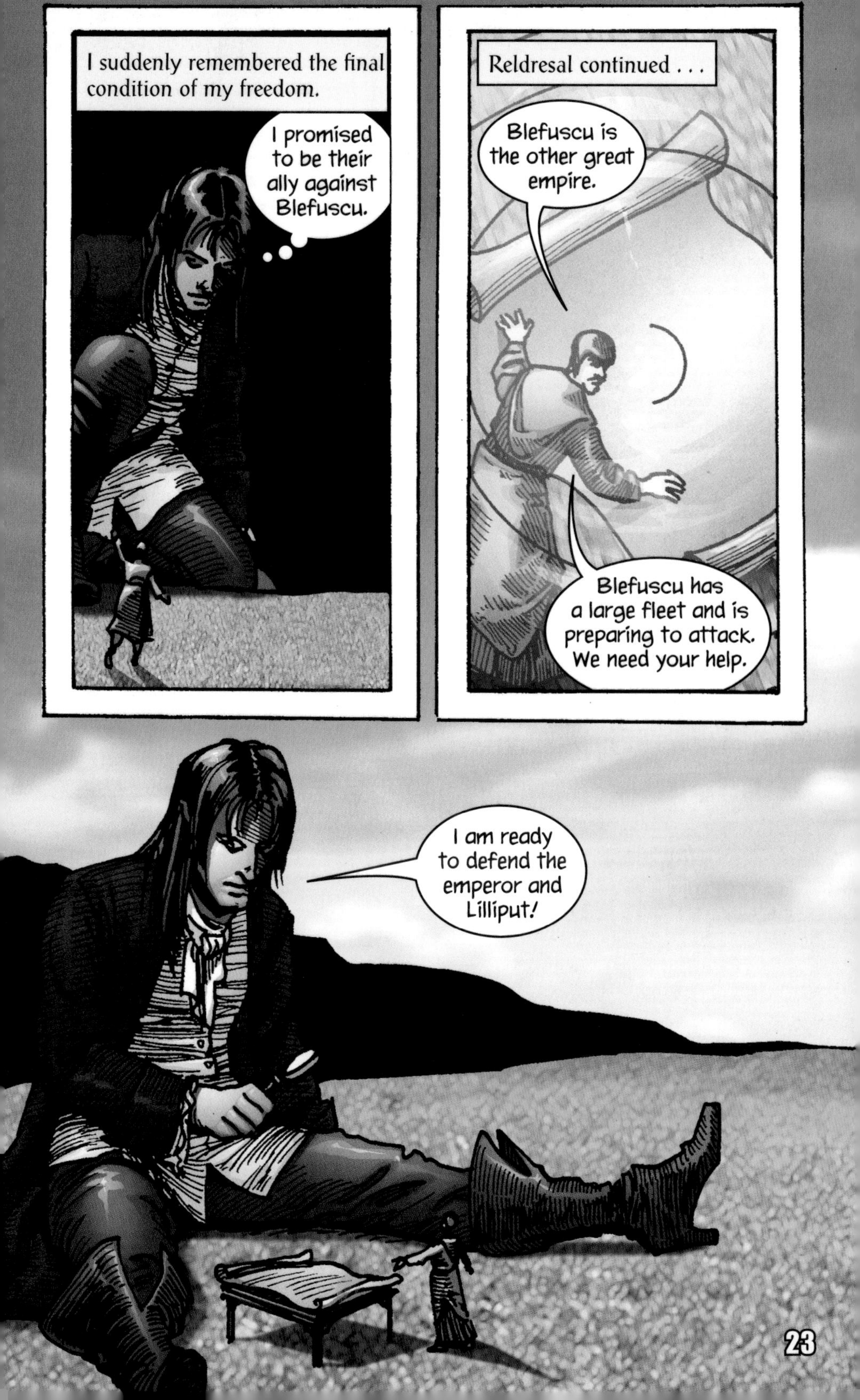
I suddenly remembered the final condition of my freedom.
I promised to be their ally against Blefuscu.
Reldresal continued . . .
Blefuscu is the other great empire.
Blefuscu has a large fleet and is preparing to attack. We need your help.
I am ready to defend the emperor and Lilliput!

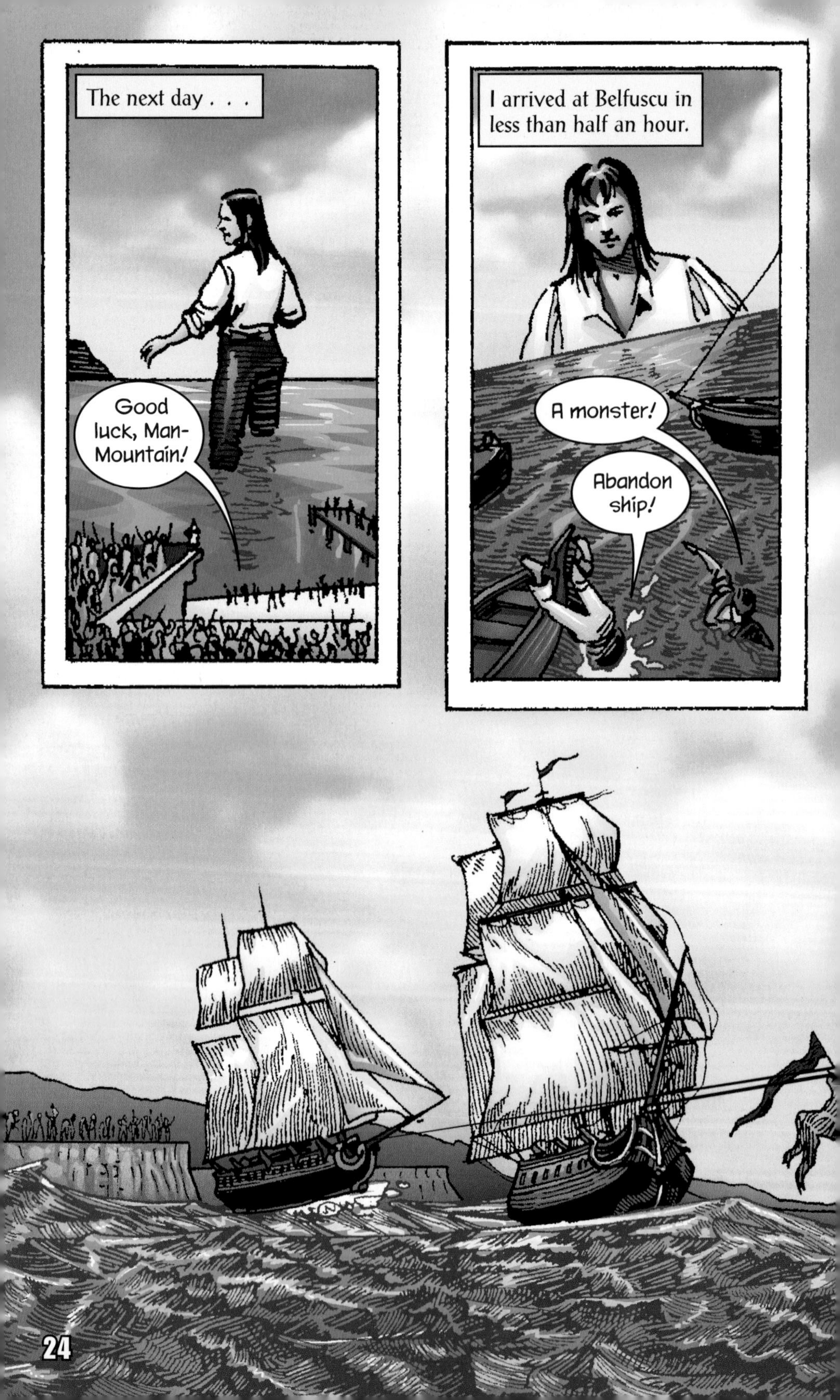
The next day . . .
Good luck, Man-Mountain!
I arrived at Belfuscu in less than half an hour.
A monster!
Abandon ship!

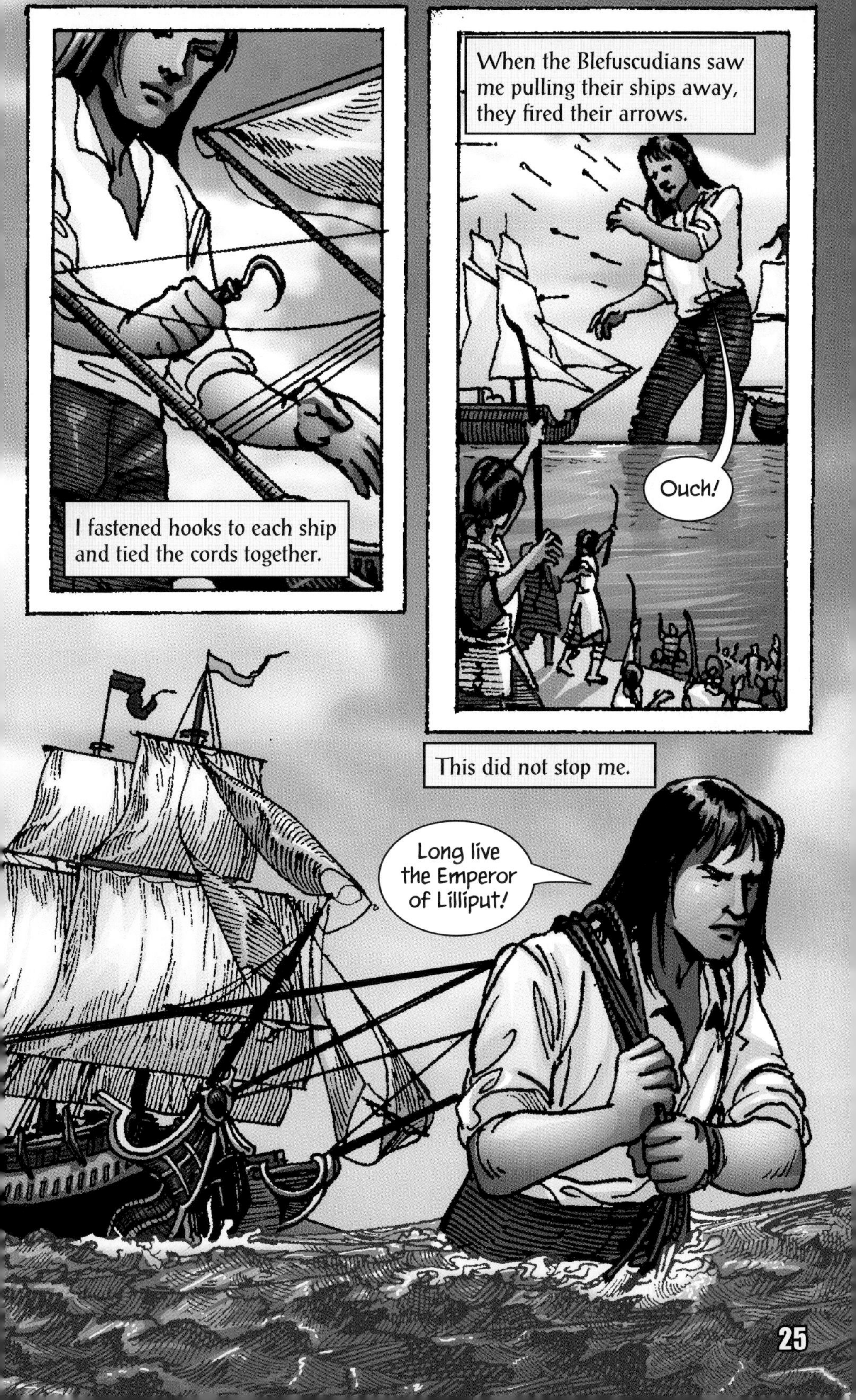
I fastened hooks to each ship and tied the cords together.
When the Blefuscudians saw me pulling their ships away, they fired their arrows.
Ouch!
This did not stop me.
Long live the Emperor of Lilliput!

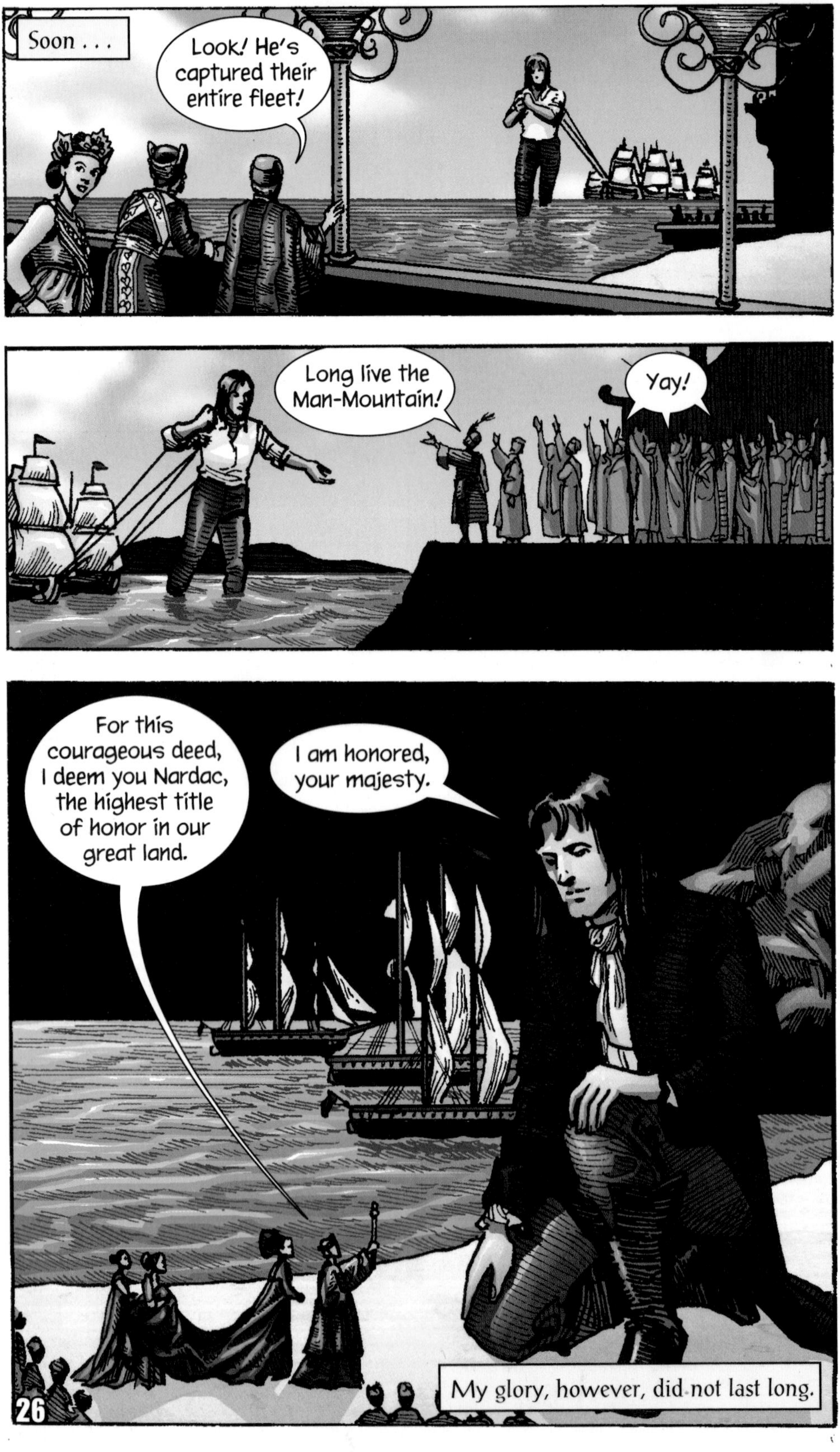

Soon . . .
Look! He's captured their entire fleet!
Long live the Man-Mountain!
Yay!
For this courageous deed, I deem you Nardac, the highest title of honor in our great land.
I am honored, your majesty.
My glory, however, did not last long.

27

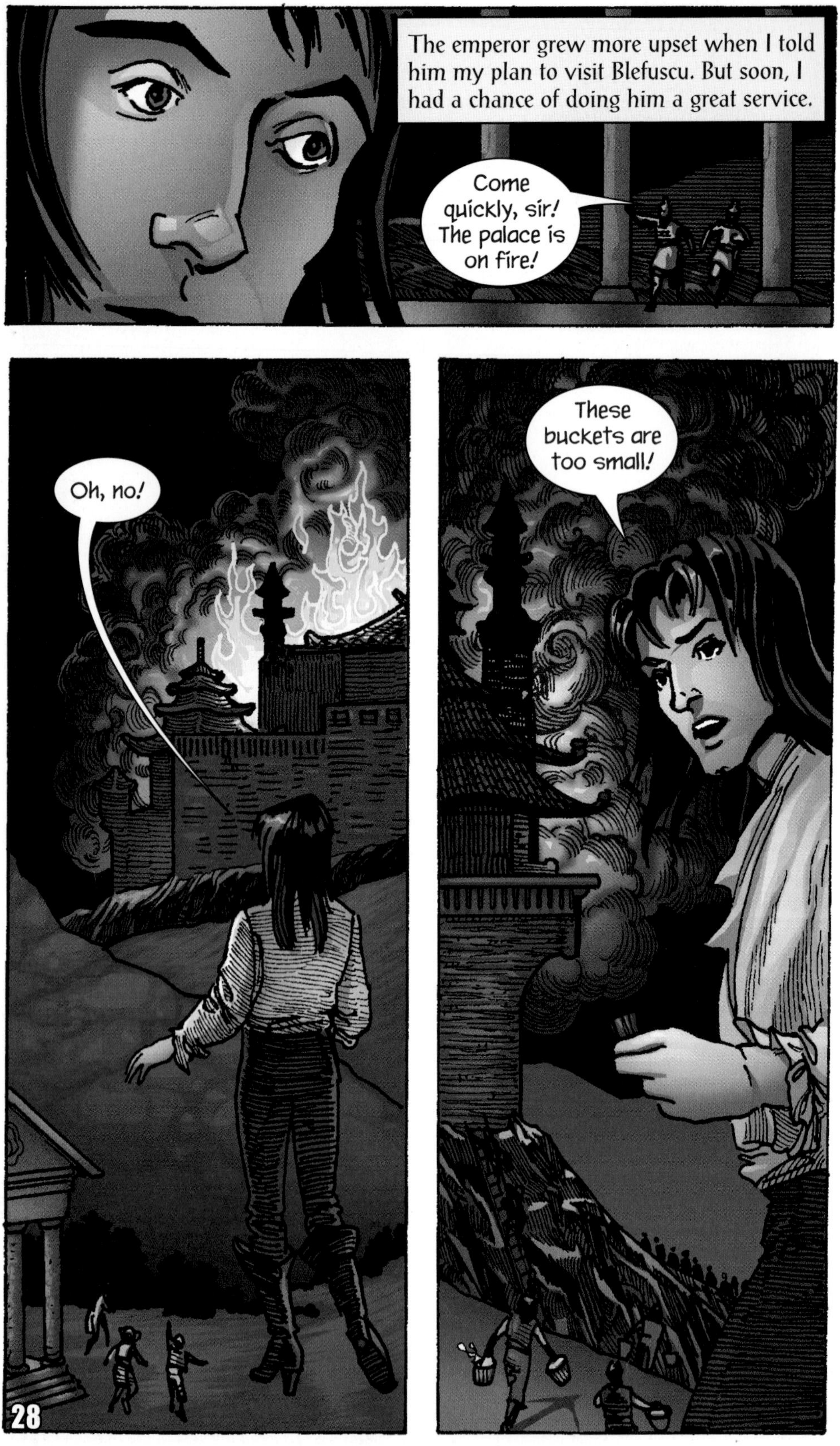
The emperor grew more upset when I told him my plan to visit Blefuscu. But soon, I had a chance of doing him a great service.
Come quickly, sir! The palace is on fire!
Oh, no!
These buckets are too small!

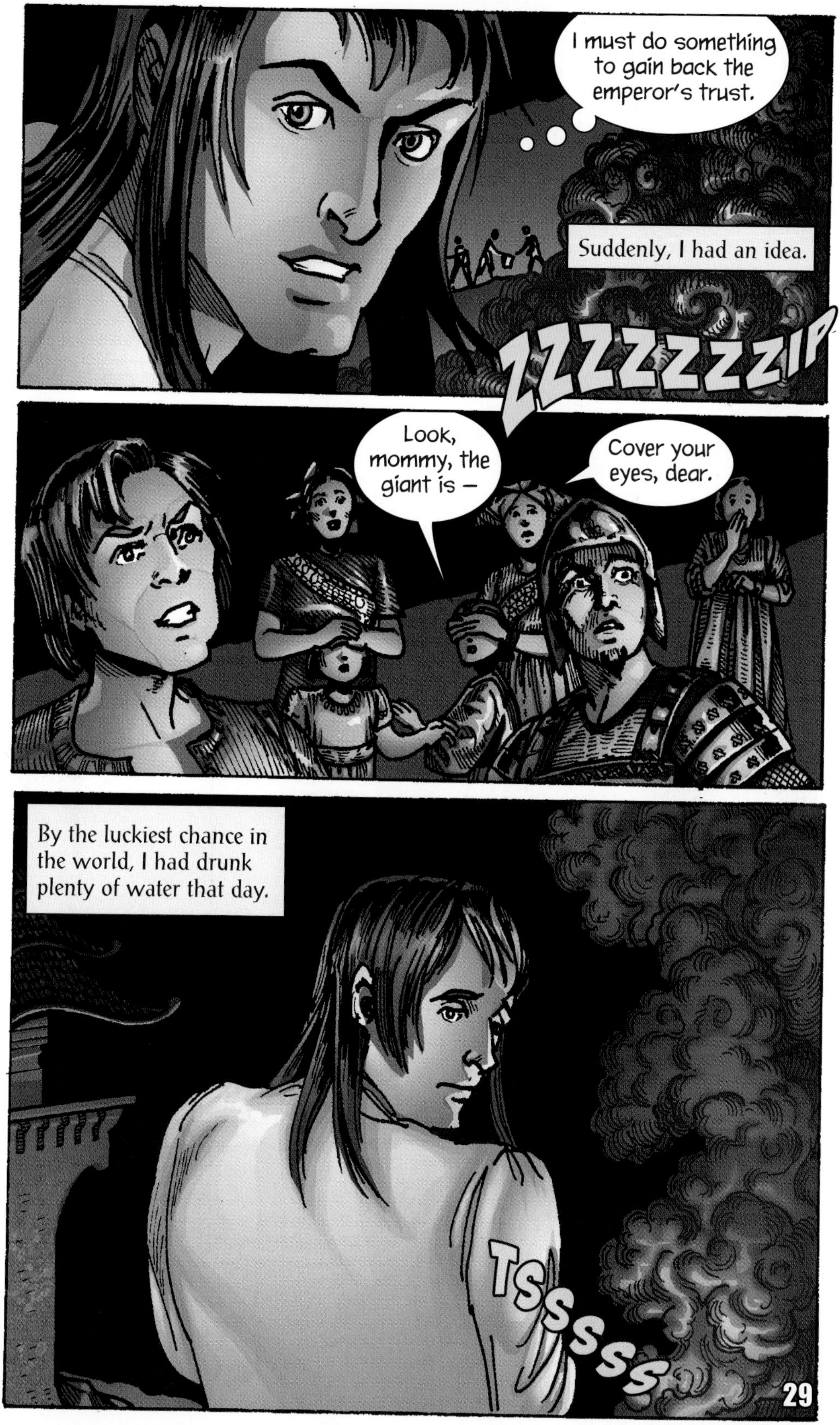
I must do something to gain back the emperor's trust.
Suddenly, I had an idea.
ZZZZZZZZIP
Look, mommy, the giant is —
Cover your eyes, dear.
By the luckiest chance in the world, I had drunk plenty of water that day.
TSSSSSS

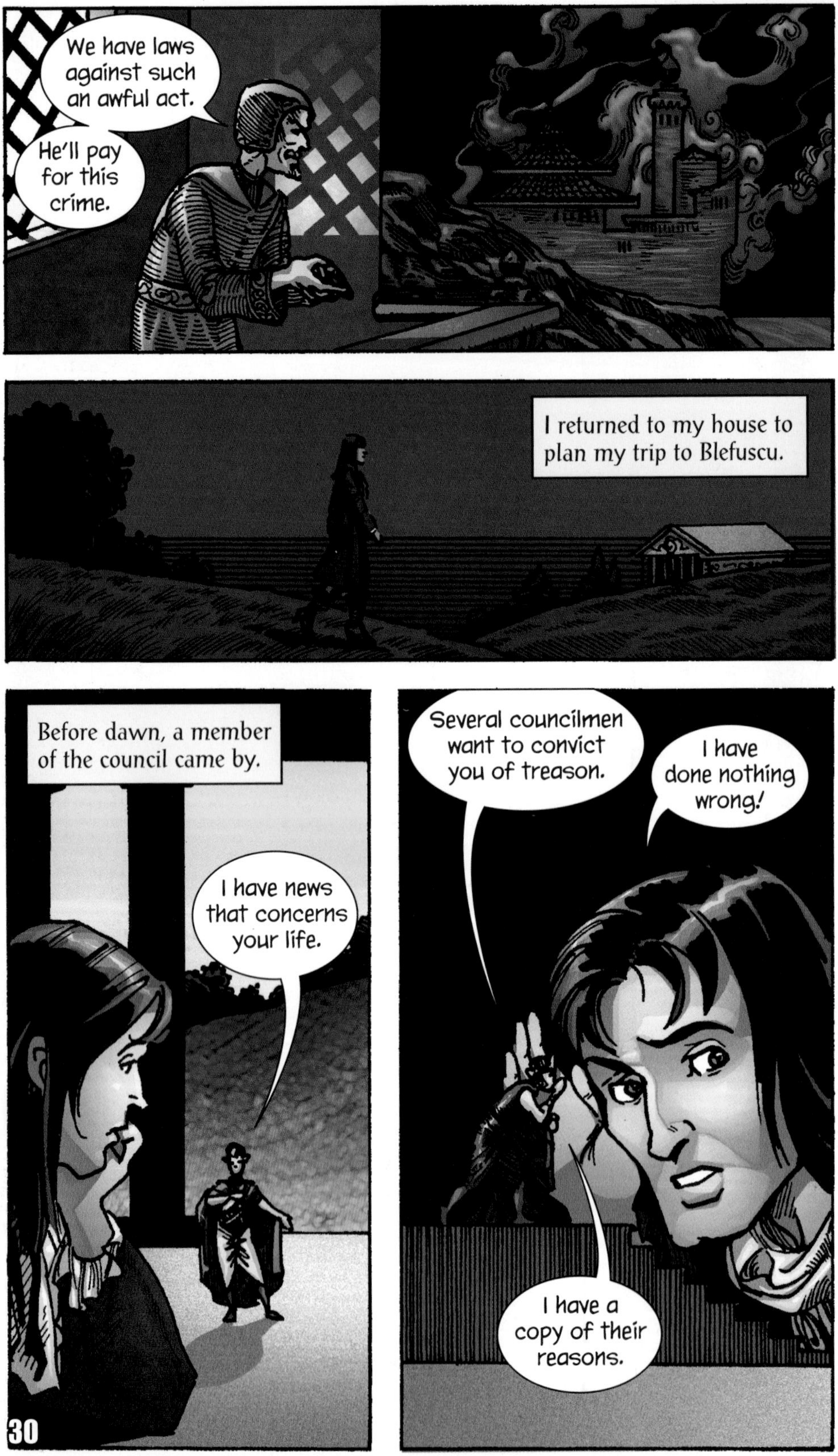
We have laws against such an awful act.
He'll pay for this crime.
I returned to my house to plan my trip to Blefuscu.
Before dawn, a member of the council came by.
I have news that concerns your life.
Several councilmen want to convict you of treason.
I have done nothing wrong!
I have a copy of their reasons.

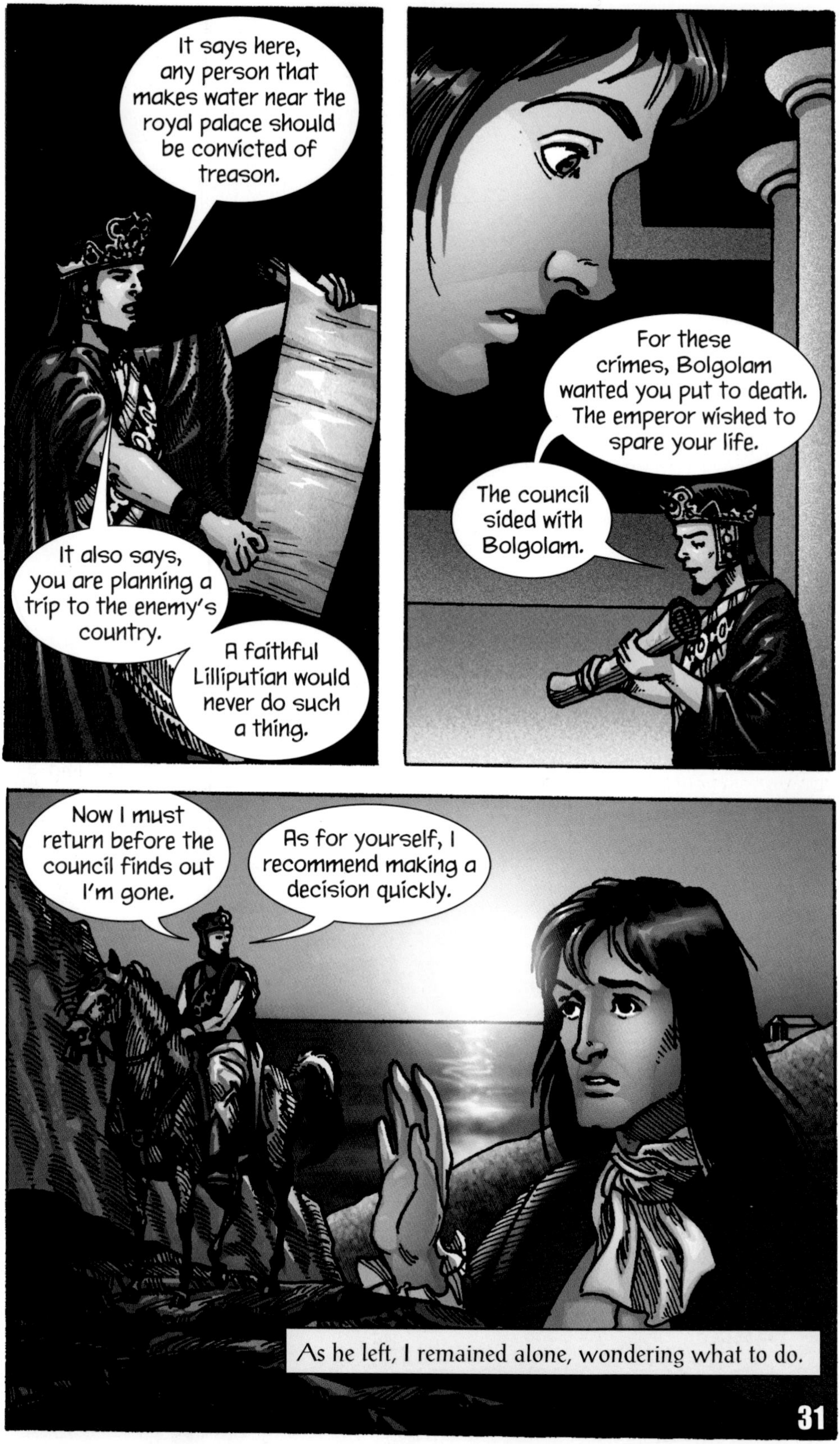
It says here, any person that makes water near the royal palace should be convicted of treason.
It also says, you are planning a trip to the enemy's country.
A faithful Lilliputian would never do such a thing.
For these crimes, Bolgolam wanted you put to death. The emperor wished to spare your life.
The council sided with Bolgolam.
Now I must return before the council finds out I'm gone.
As for yourself, I recommend making a decision quickly.
As he left, I remained alone, wondering what to do.

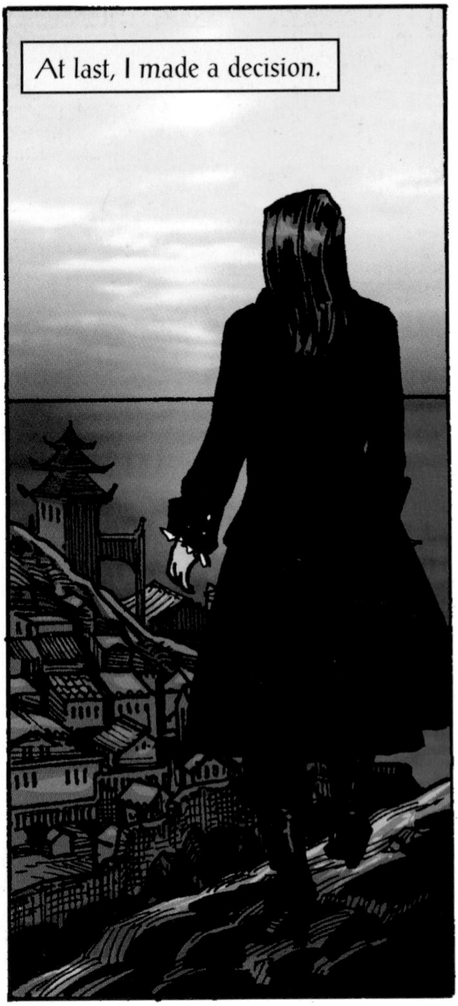
At last, I made a decision.

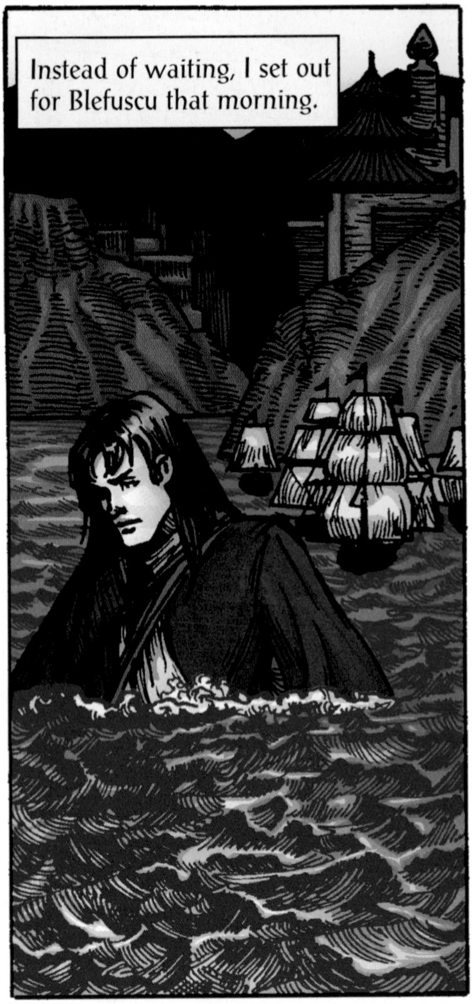
Instead of waiting, I set out for Blefuscu that morning.

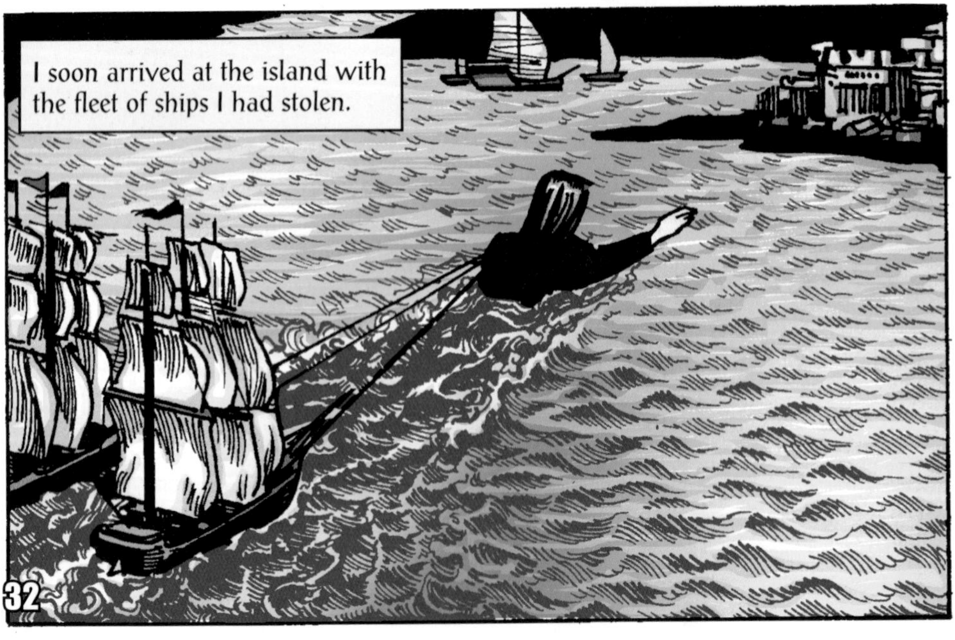
I soon arrived at the island with the fleet of ships I had stolen.

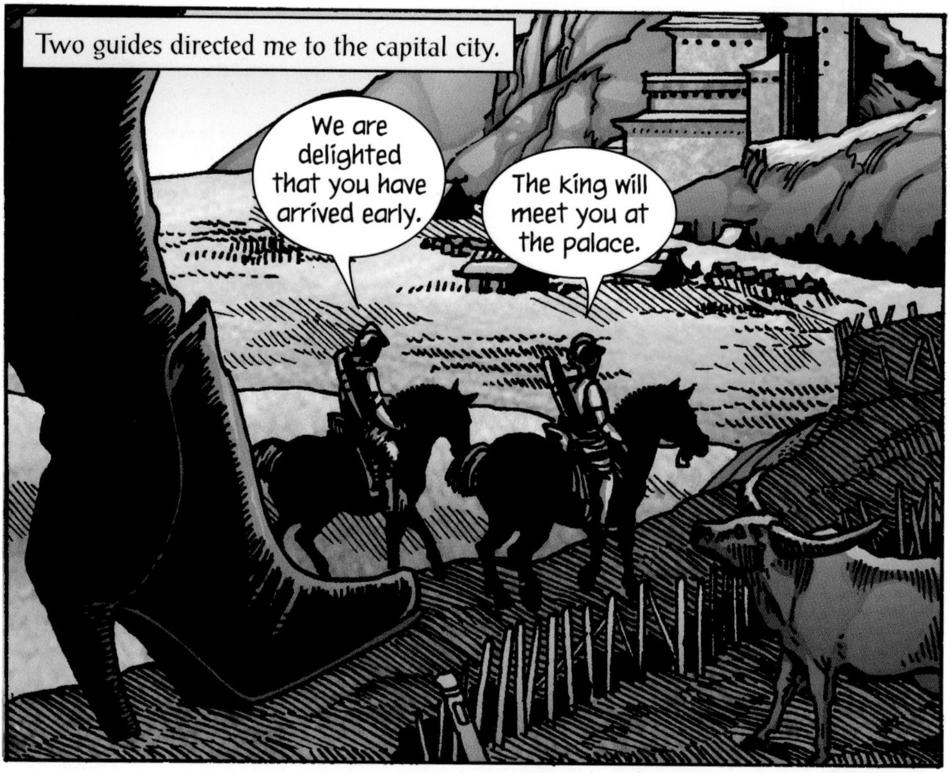
Two guides directed me to the capital city.
We are delighted that you have arrived early.
The king will meet you at the palace.

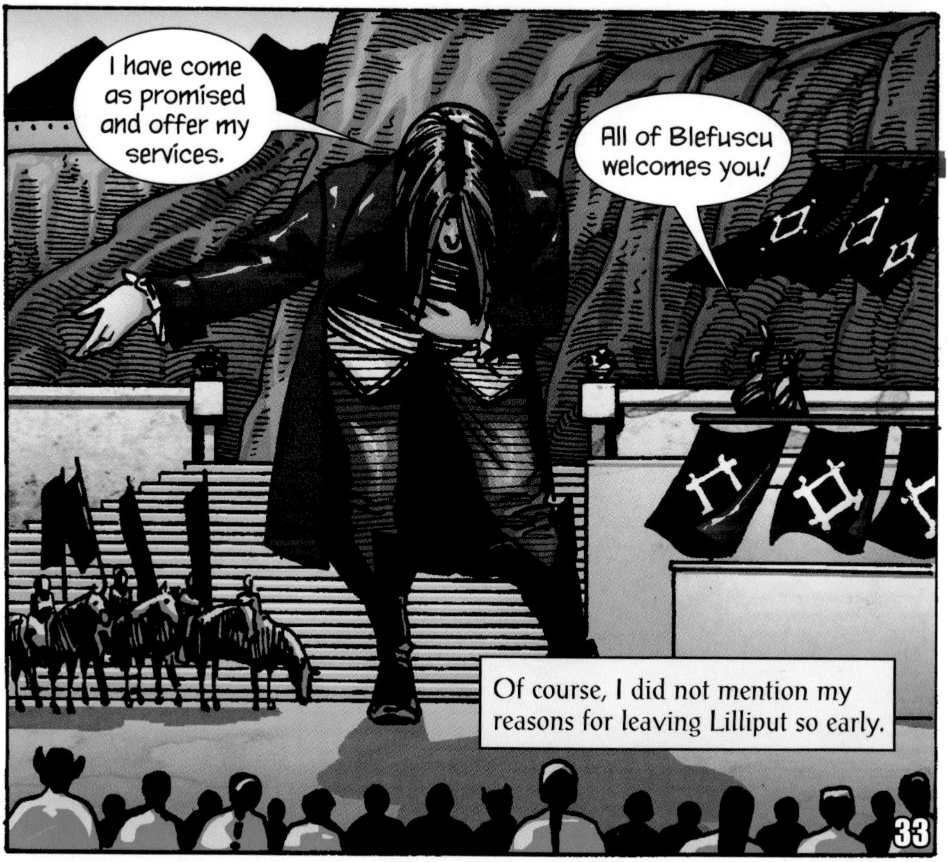
I have come as promised and offer my services.
All of Blefuscu welcomes you!
Of course, I did not mention my reasons for leaving Lilliput so early.

CHAPTER 4:
LAND OF GIANTS

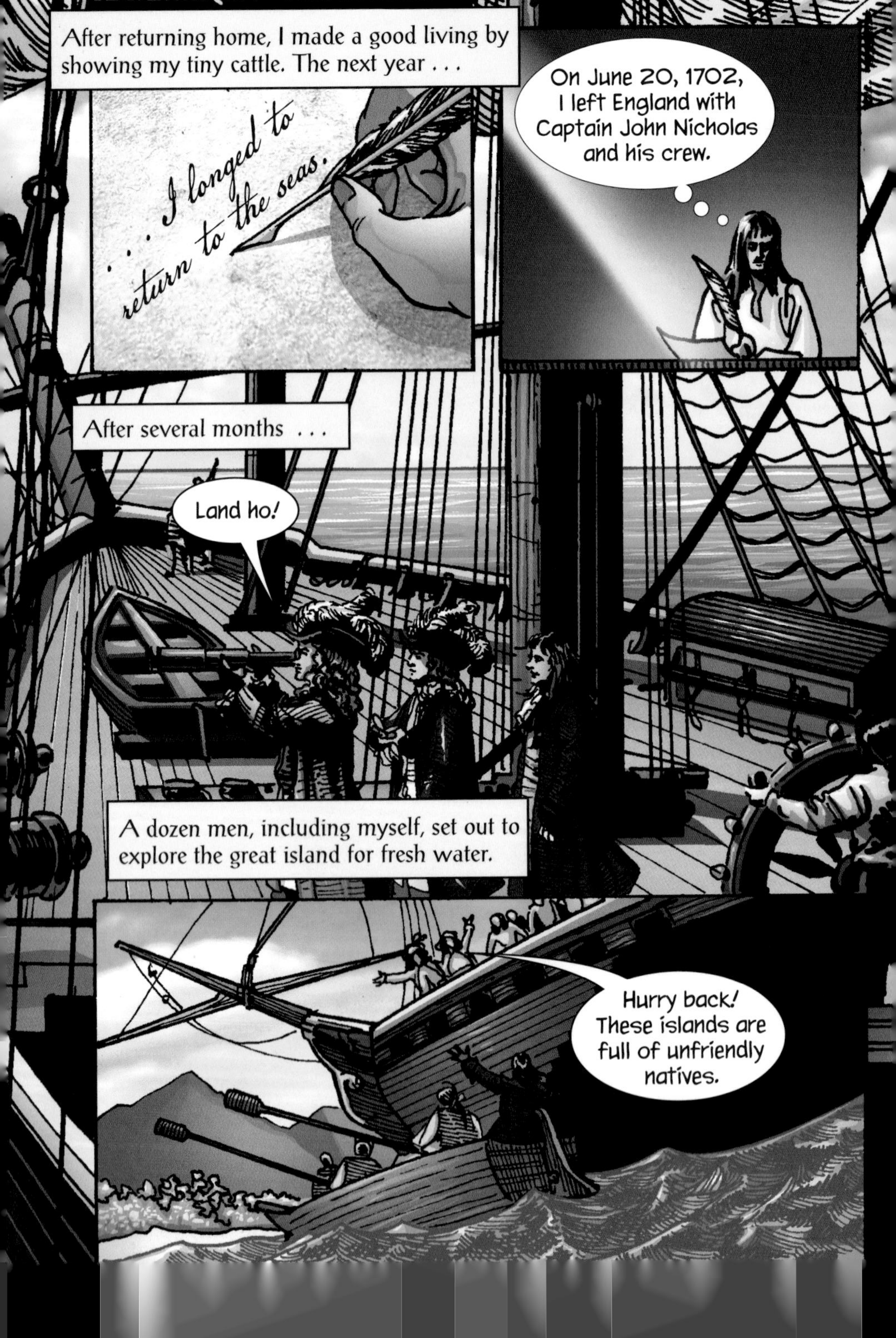
After returning home, I made a good living by showing my tiny cattle. The next year . . .
. . . I longed to return to the seas.
On June 20, 1702, I left England with Captain John Nicholas and his crew.
After several months . . .
Land ho!
A dozen men, including myself, set out to explore the great island for fresh water.
Hurry back! These islands are full of unfriendly natives.

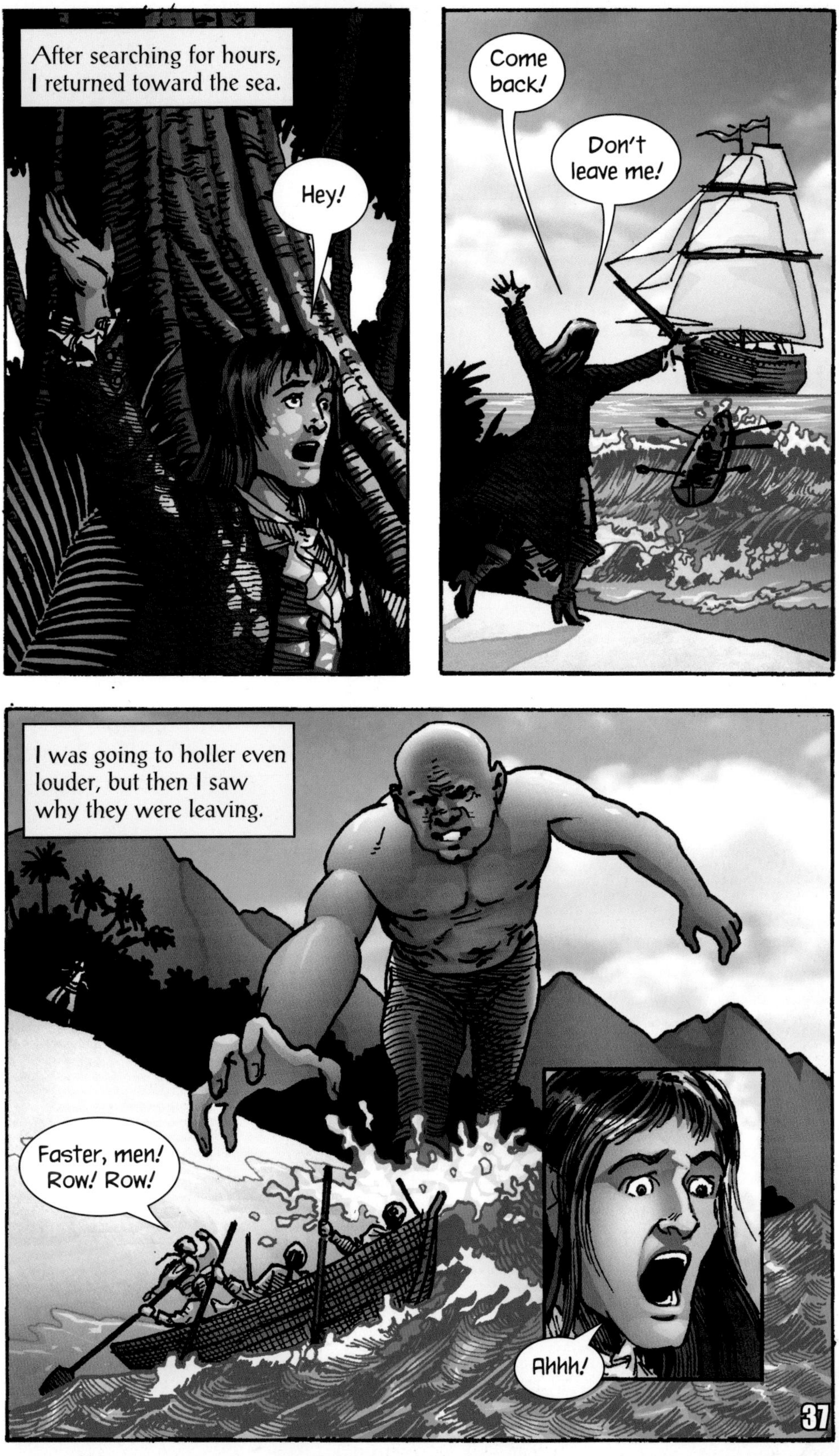
After searching for hours, I returned toward the sea.
Hey!
Come back!
Don't leave me!
I was going to holler even louder, but then I saw why they were leaving.
Faster, men! Row! Row!
Ahhh!

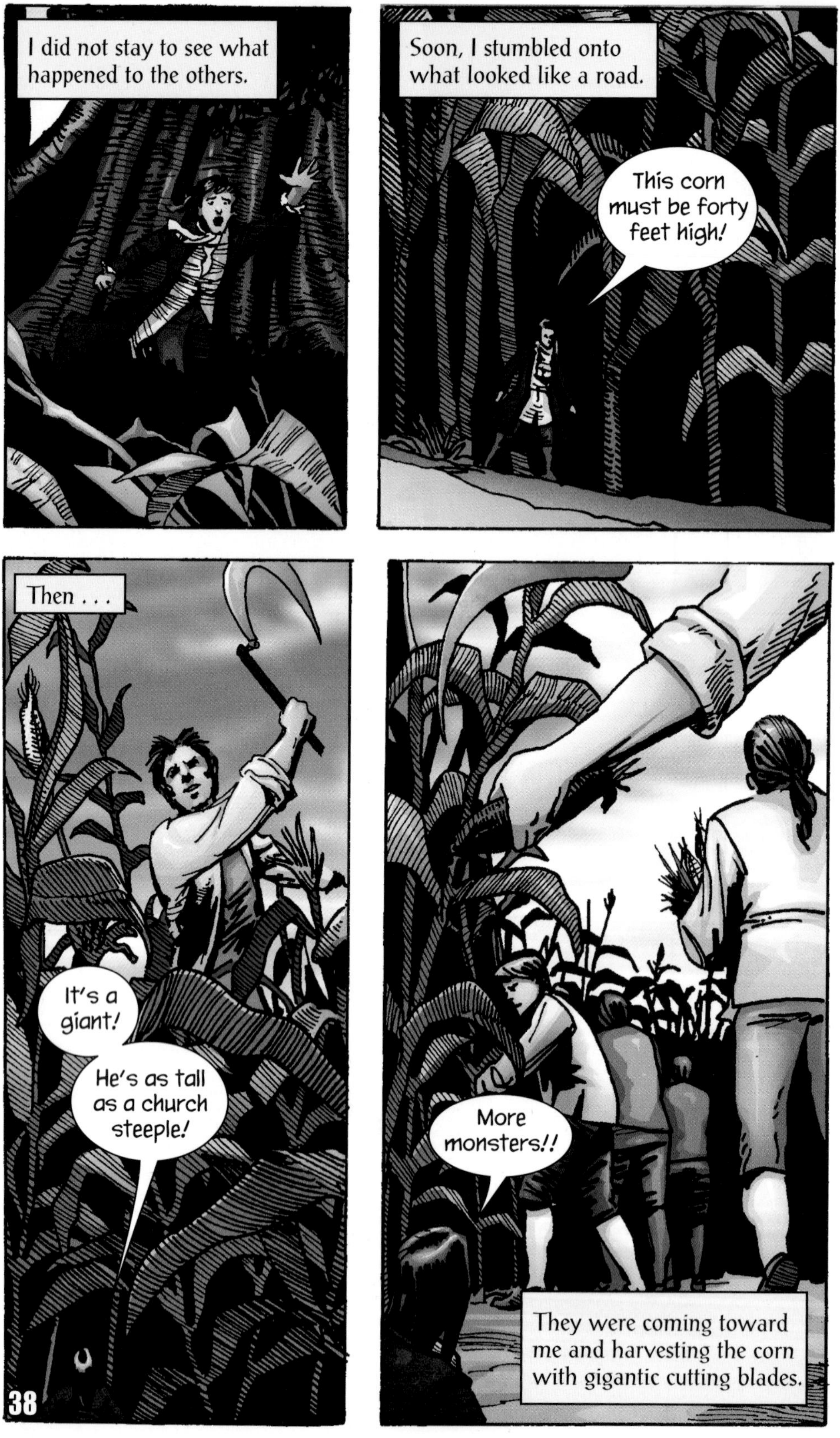
I did not stay to see what happened to the others.
Soon, I stumbled onto what looked like a road.
This corn must be forty feet high!
Then . . .
It's a giant!
He's as tall as a church steeple!
More monsters!!
They were coming toward me and harvesting the corn with gigantic cutting blades.

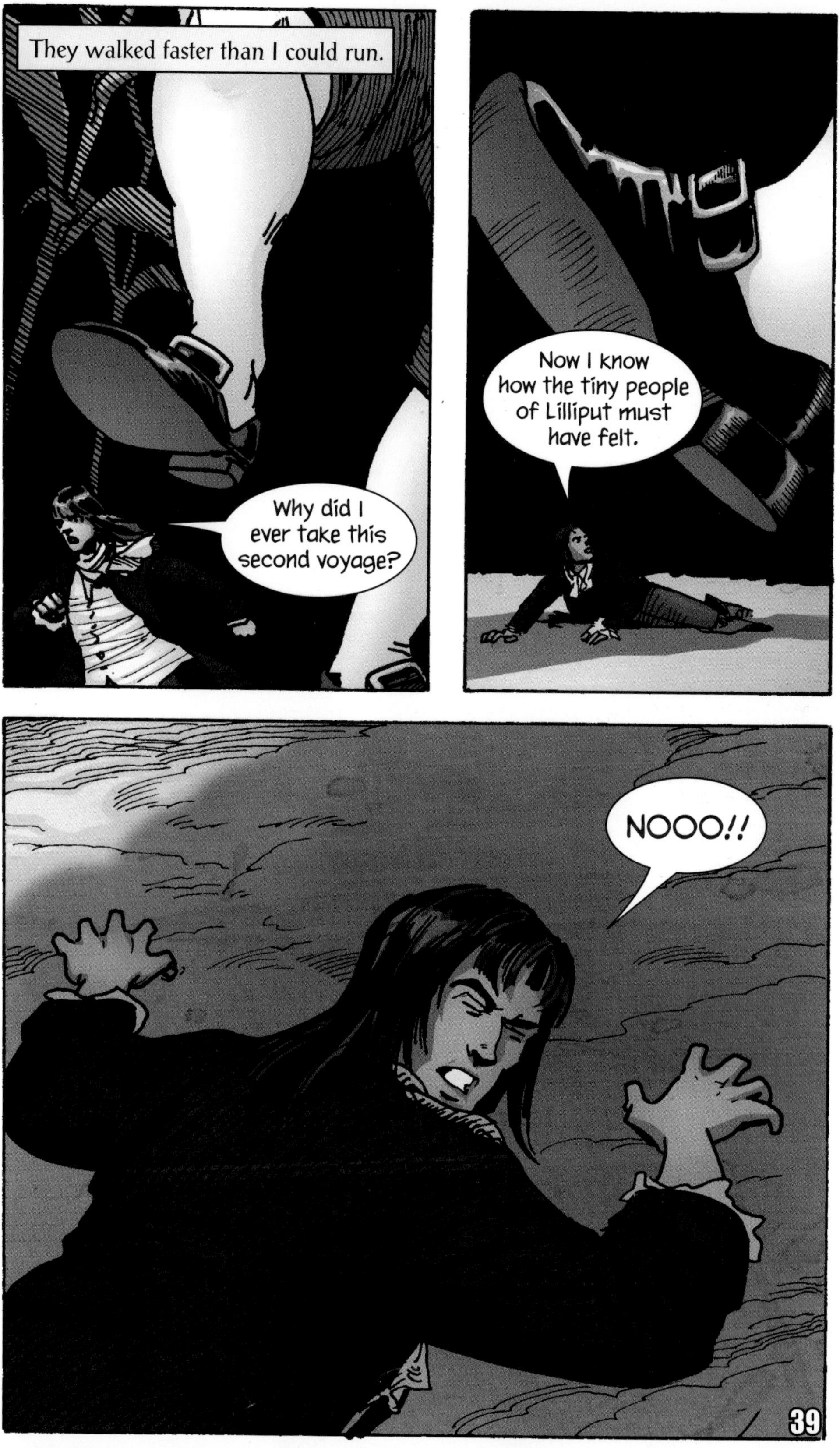
They walked faster than I could run.
Why did I ever take this second voyage?
Now I know how the tiny people of Lilliput must have felt.
NOOO!!

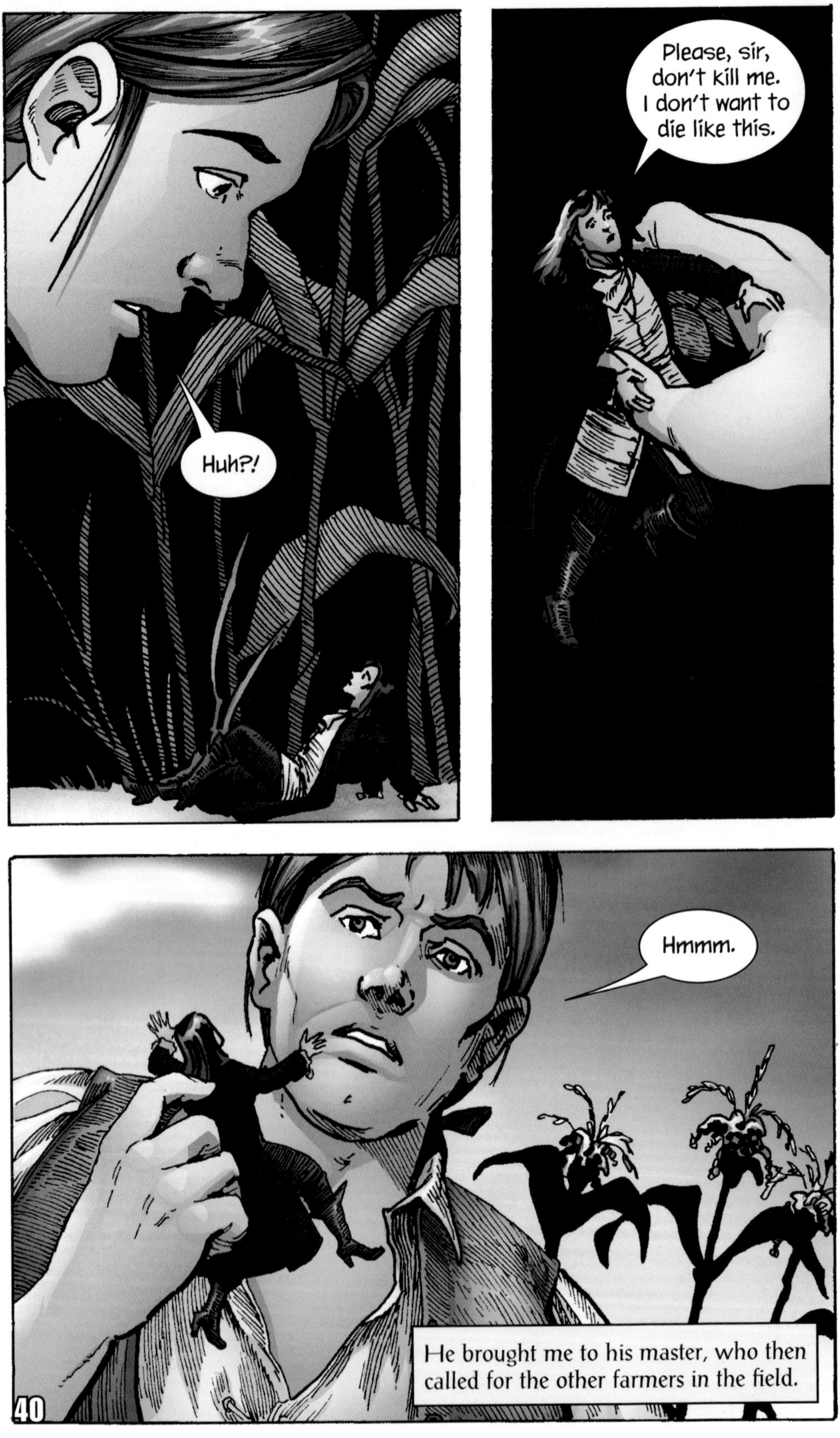
Huh?!
Please, sir, don't kill me. I don't want to die like this.
Hmmm.
He brought me to his master, who then called for the other farmers in the field.

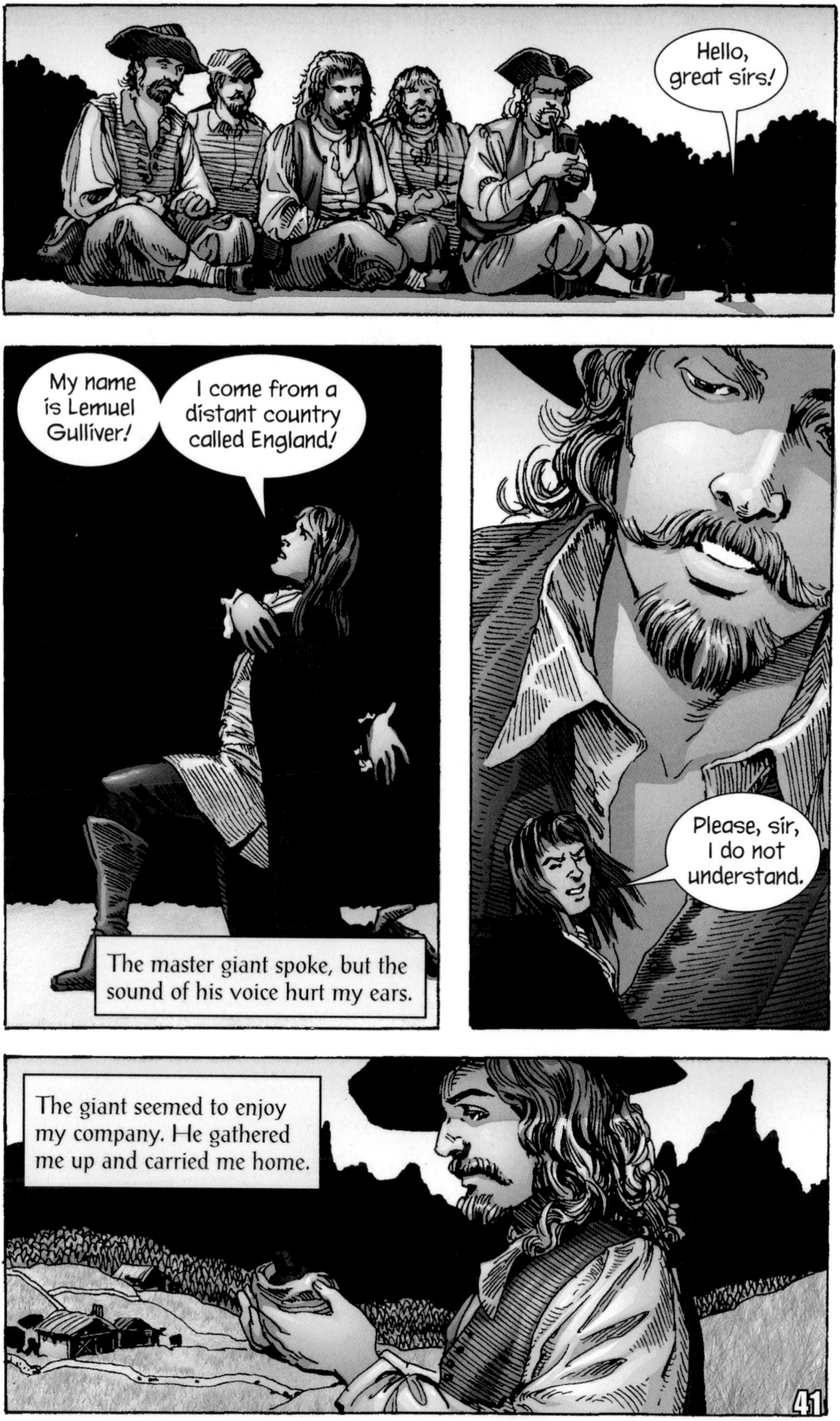
Hello, great sirs!
My name is Lemuel Gulliver!
I come from a distant country called England!
The master giant spoke, but the sound of his voice hurt my ears.
Please, sir, I do not understand.
The giant seemed to enjoy my company. He gathered me up and carried me home.

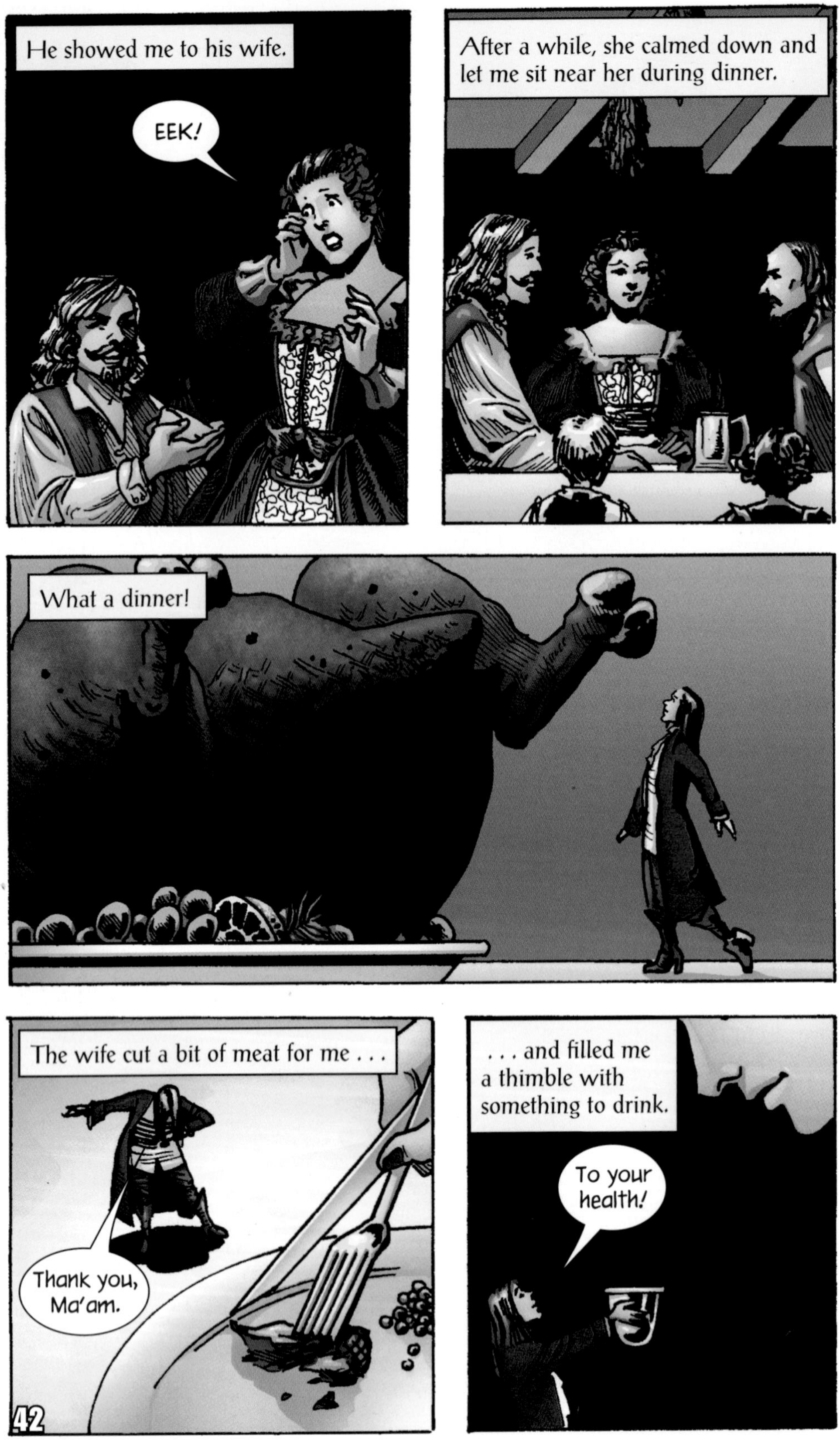
He showed me to his wife.
EEK!
After a while, she calmed down and let me sit near her during dinner.
What a dinner!
The wife cut a bit of meat for me . . .
Thank you, Ma'am.
. . . and filled me a thimble with something to drink.
To your health!

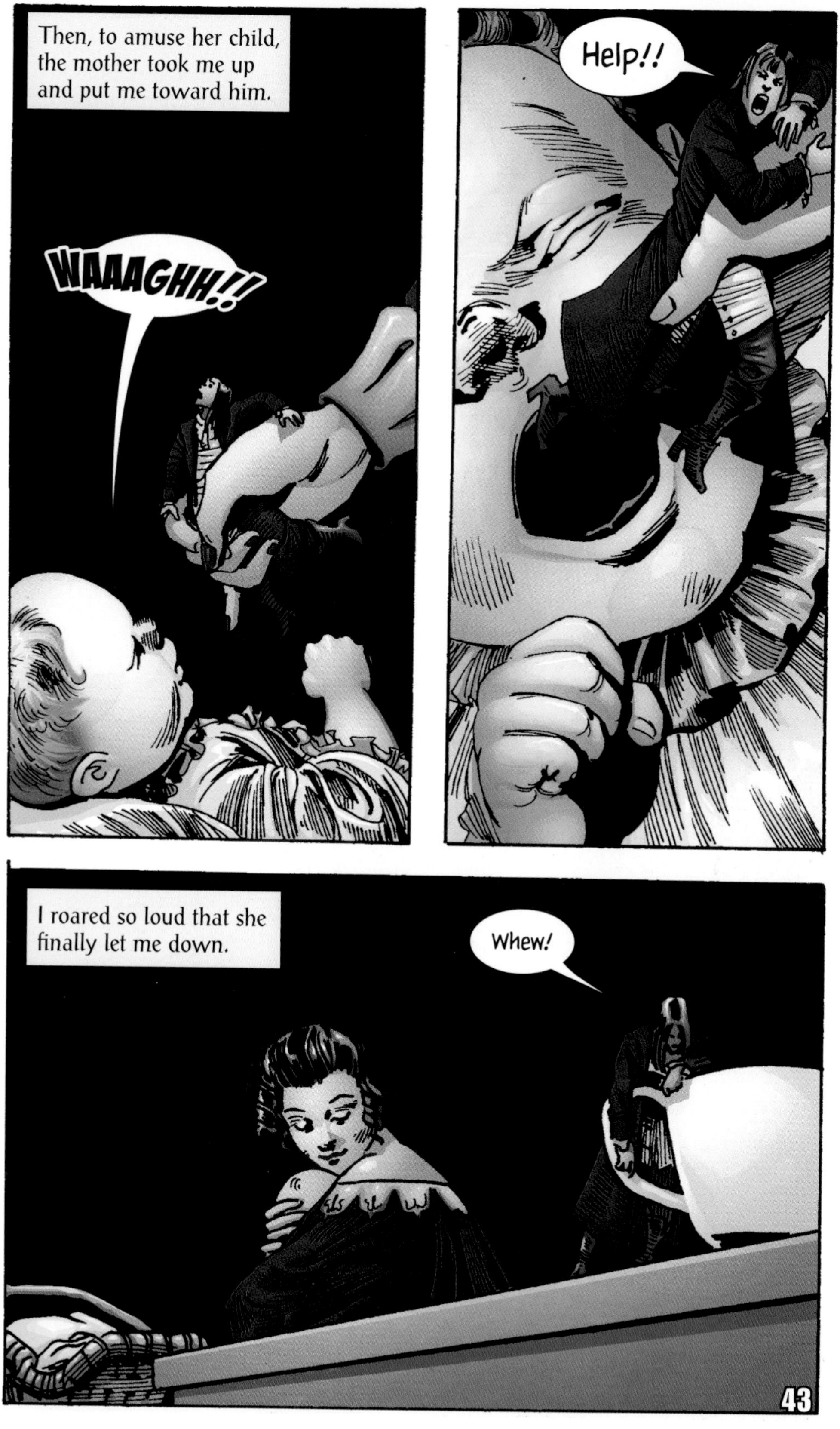
Then, to amuse her child, the mother took me up and put me toward him.
WAAAGHH!!
Help!!
I roared so loud that she finally let me down.
Whew!

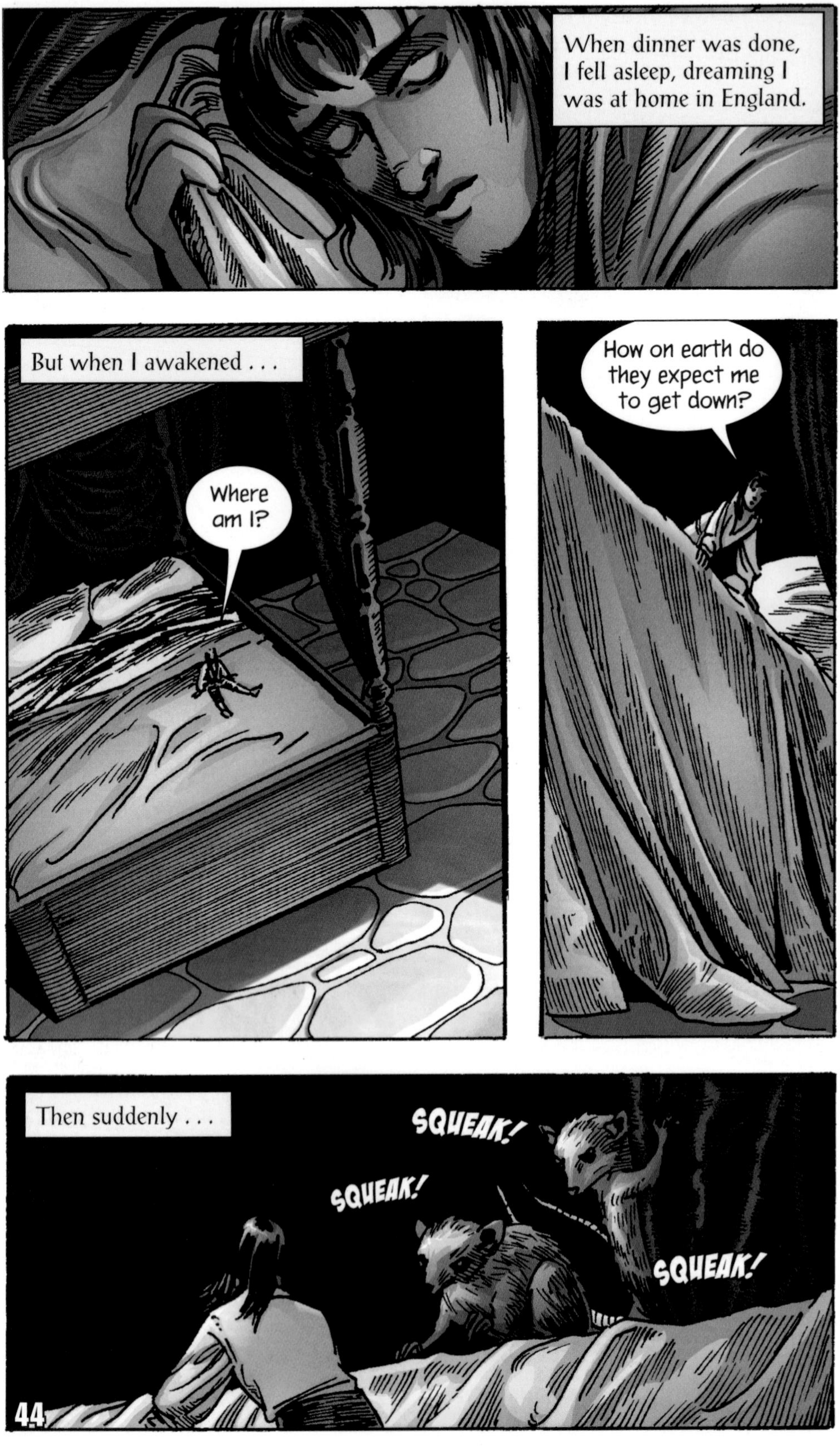
When dinner was done, I fell asleep, dreaming I was at home in England.
But when I awakened . . .
Where am I?
How on earth do they expect me to get down?
Then suddenly . . .
SQUEAK!
SQUEAK!
SQUEAK!

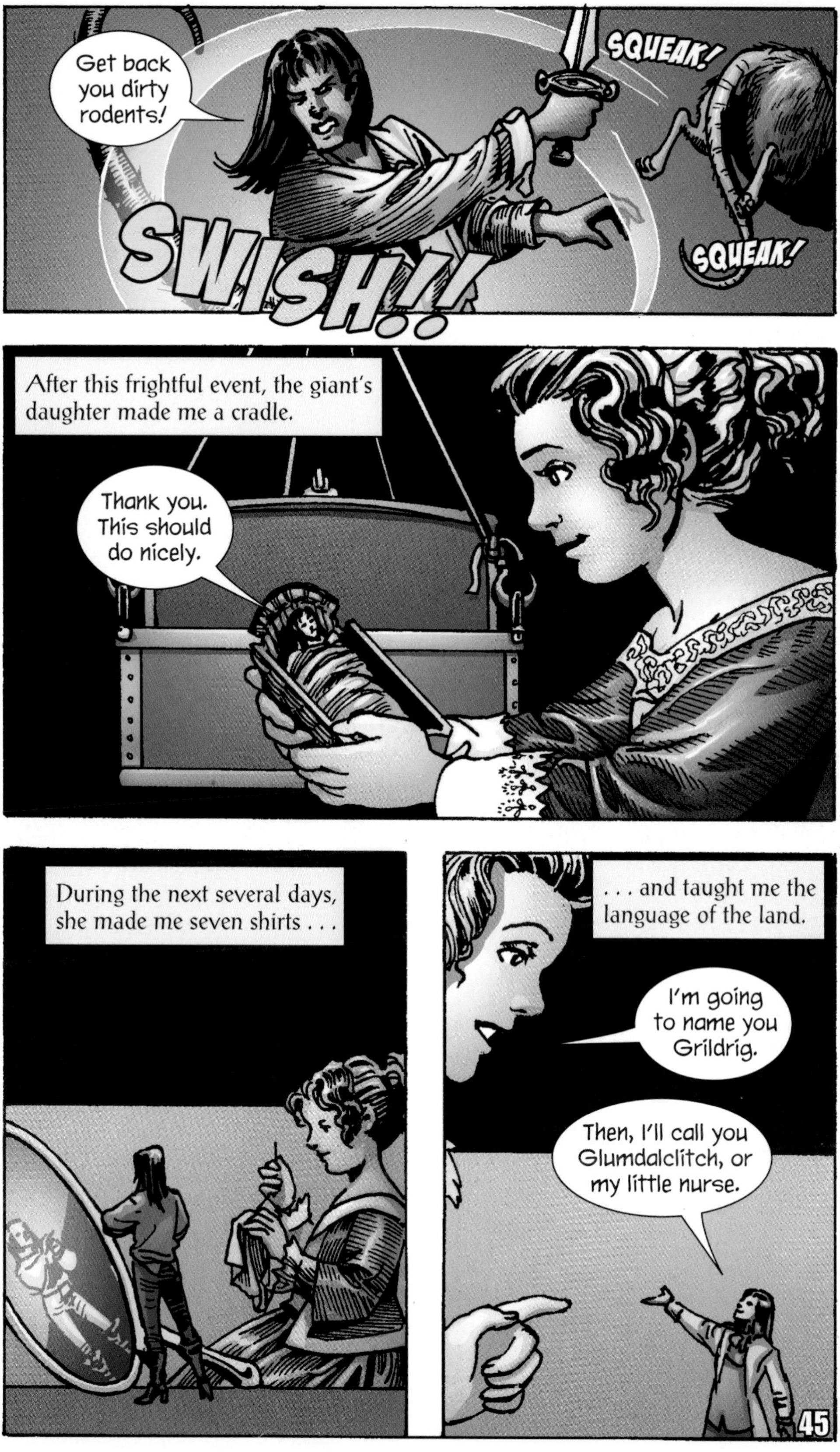
Get back you dirty rodents!
SQUEAK!
SWISH!!
SQUEAK!
After this frightful event, the giant's daughter made me a cradle.
Thank you. This should do nicely.
During the next several days, she made me seven shirts . . .
. . . and taught me the language of the land.
I'm going to name you Grildrig.
Then, I'll call you Glumdalclitch, or my little nurse.

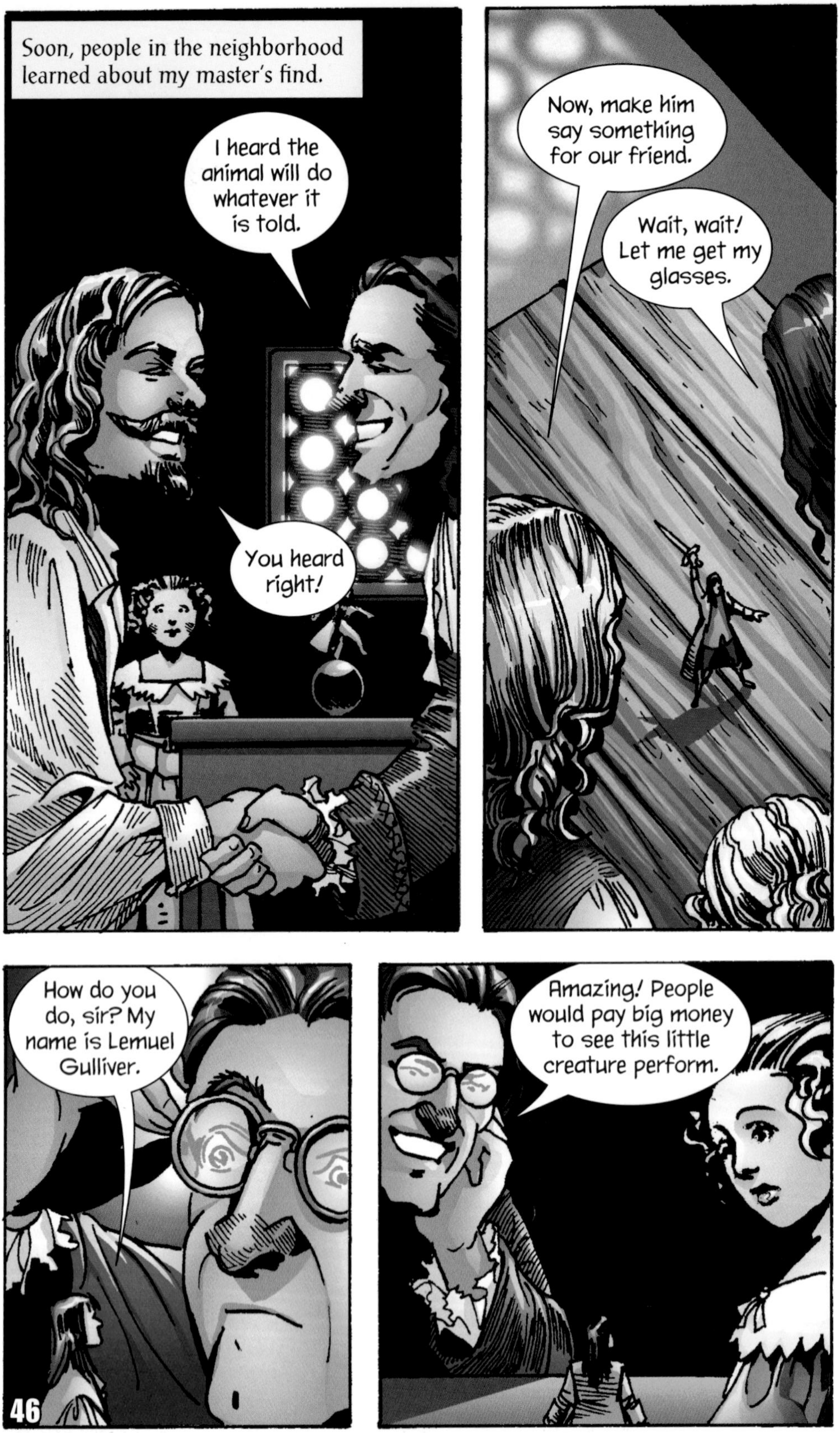
Soon, people in the neighborhood learned about my master's find.
I heard the animal will do whatever it is told.
You heard right!
Now, make him say something for our friend.
Wait, wait! Let me get my glasses.
How do you do, sir? My name is Lemuel Gulliver.
Amazing! People would pay big money to see this little creature perform.

The next day, my master carried me in a box to the neighboring town.

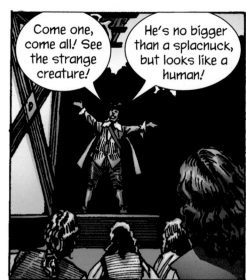

Come one, come all! See the strange creature!

He's no bigger than a splacnuck, but looks like a human!

Okay, Grildrig, remember what I taught you.

My name is Lemuel Gulliver.

My master wanted to take the show on the road and make more money.

But Father, Grildrig is too tired to perform.

He'll do what he's told!

47

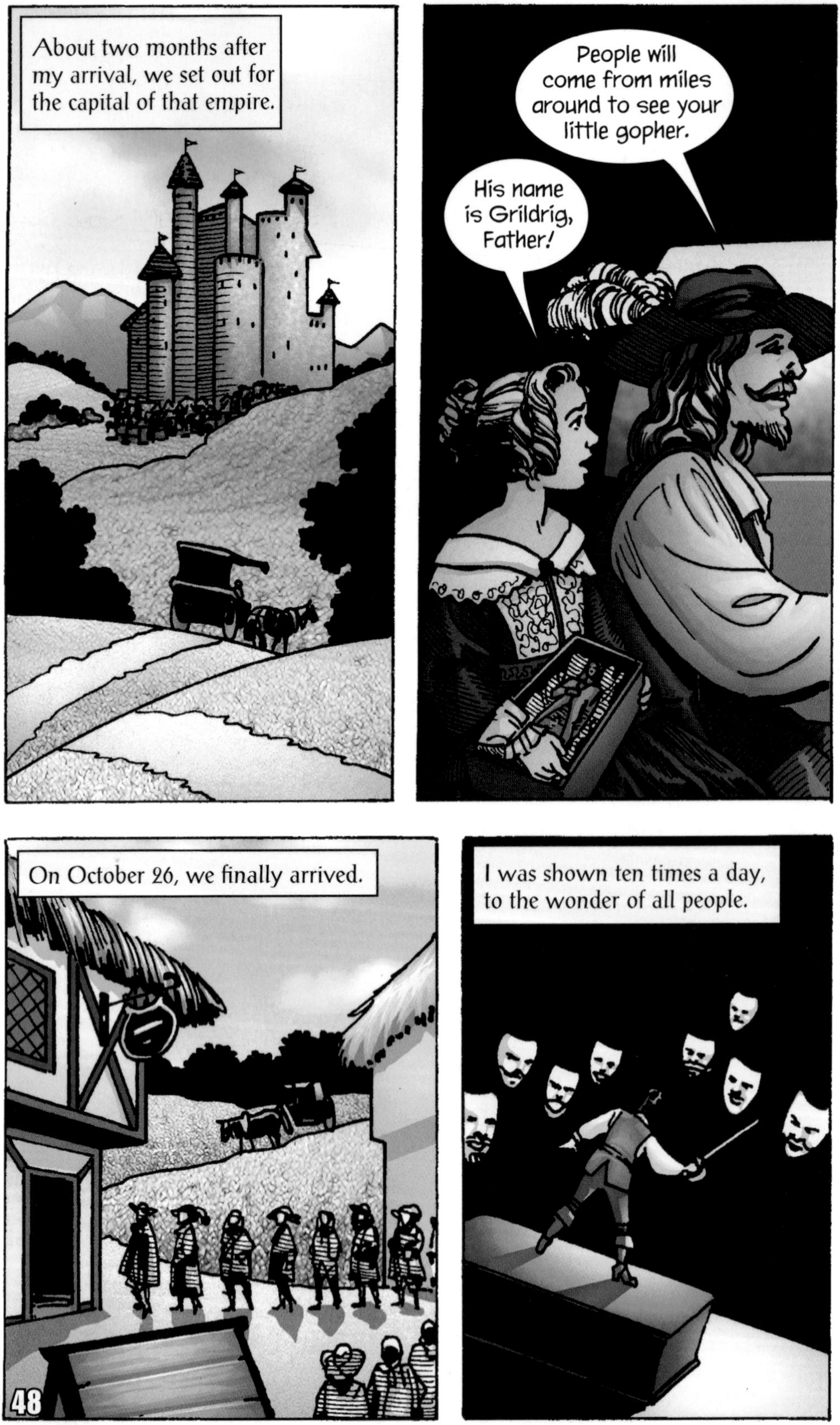
About two months after my arrival, we set out for the capital of that empire.
People will come from miles around to see your little gopher.
His name is Grildrig, Father!
On October 26, we finally arrived.
I was shown ten times a day, to the wonder of all people.

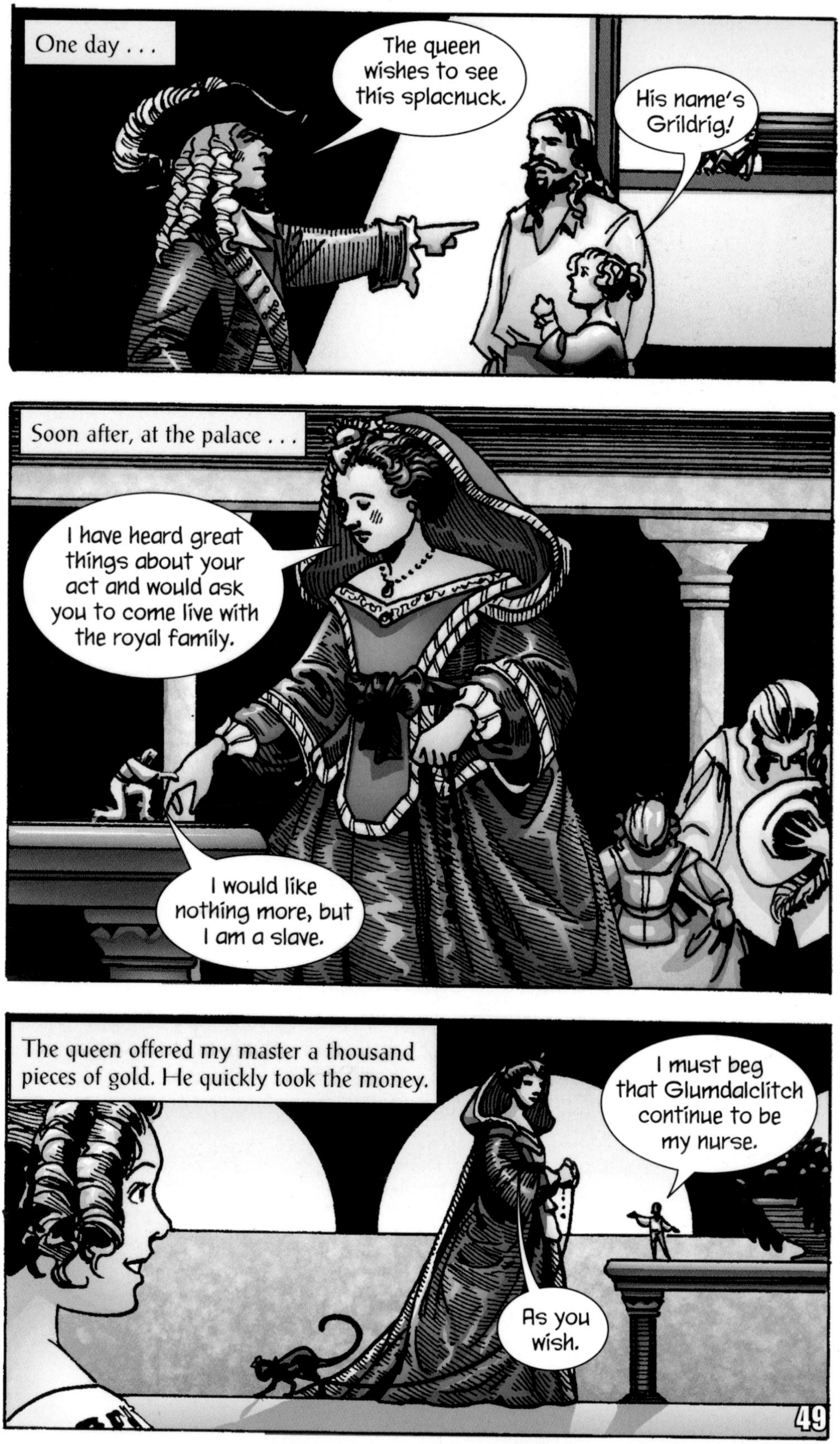

One day . . .
The queen wishes to see this splacnuck.
His name's Grildrig!
Soon after, at the palace . . .
I have heard great things about your act and would ask you to come live with the royal family.
I would like nothing more, but I am a slave.
The queen offered my master a thousand pieces of gold. He quickly took the money.
I must beg that Glumdalclitch continue to be my nurse.
As you wish.

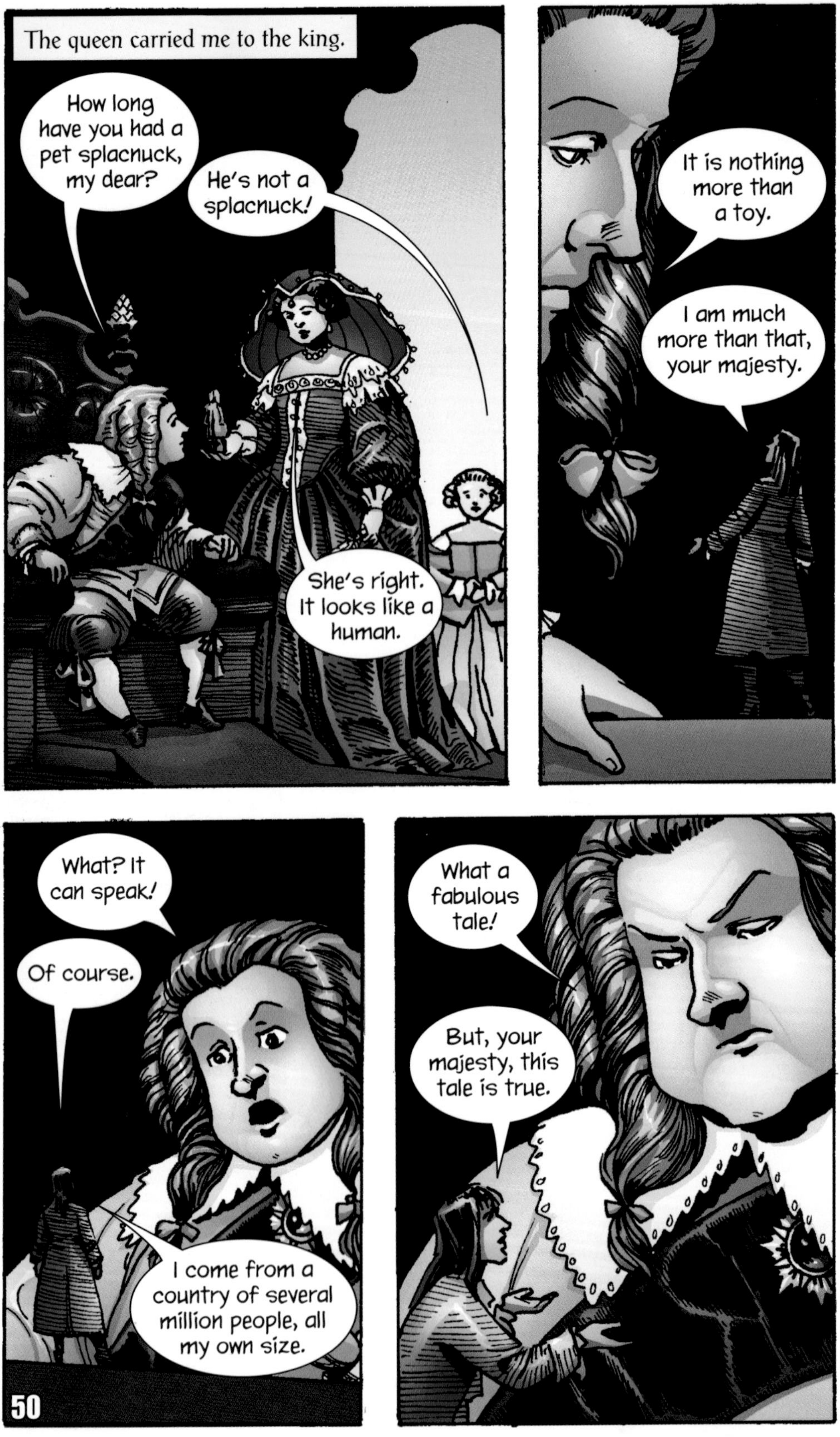
The queen carried me to the king.
How long have you had a pet splacnuck, my dear?
He's not a splacnuck!
She's right. It looks like a human.
It is nothing more than a toy.
I am much more than that, your majesty.
What? It can speak!
Of course.
I come from a country of several million people, all my own size.
What a fabulous tale!
But, your majesty, this tale is true.

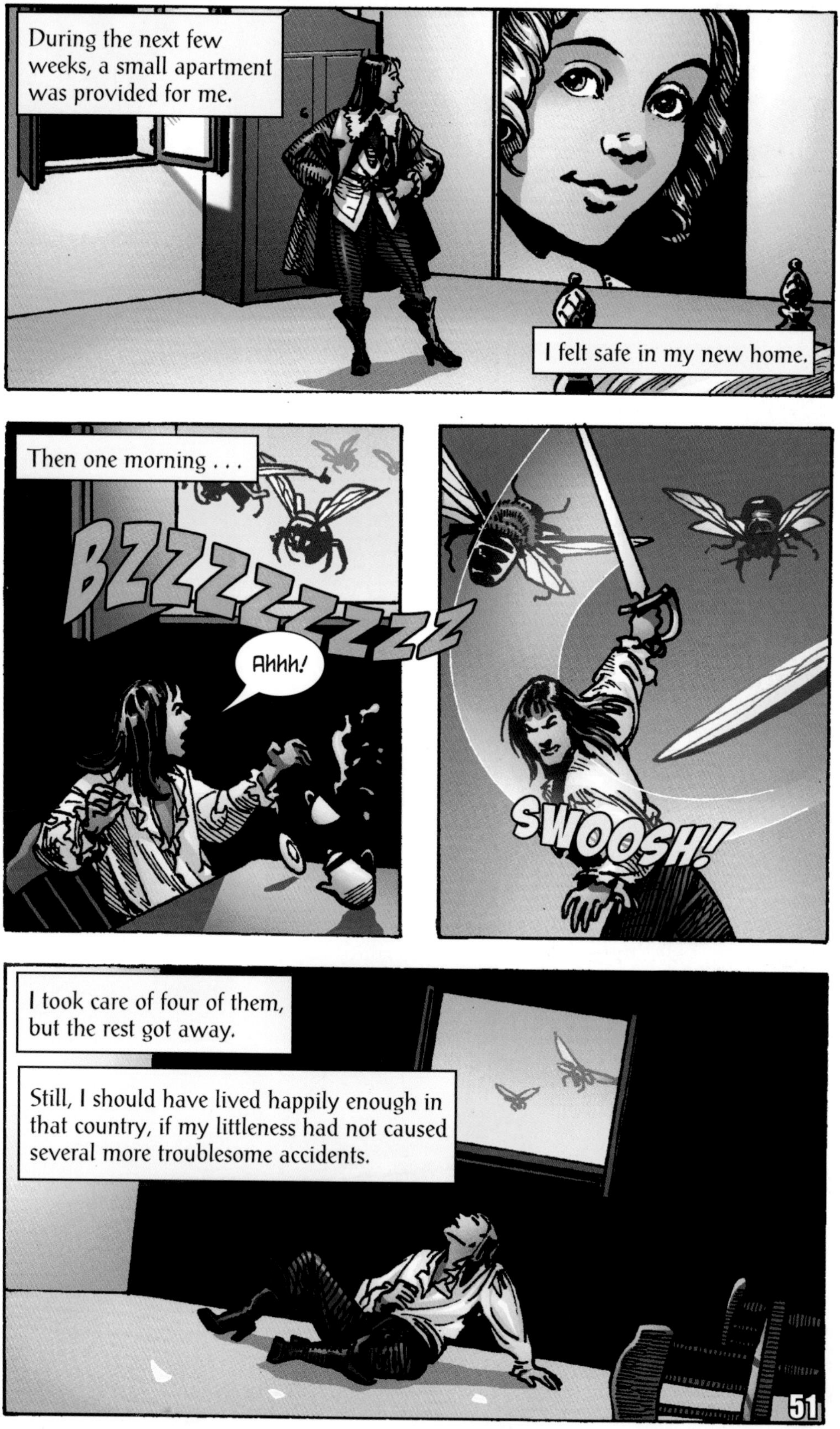
During the next few weeks, a small apartment was provided for me.
I felt safe in my new home.
Then one morning . . .
BZZZZZZZZ
Ahhh!
SWOOSH!
I took care of four of them, but the rest got away.
Still, I should have lived happily enough in that country, if my littleness had not caused several more troublesome accidents.

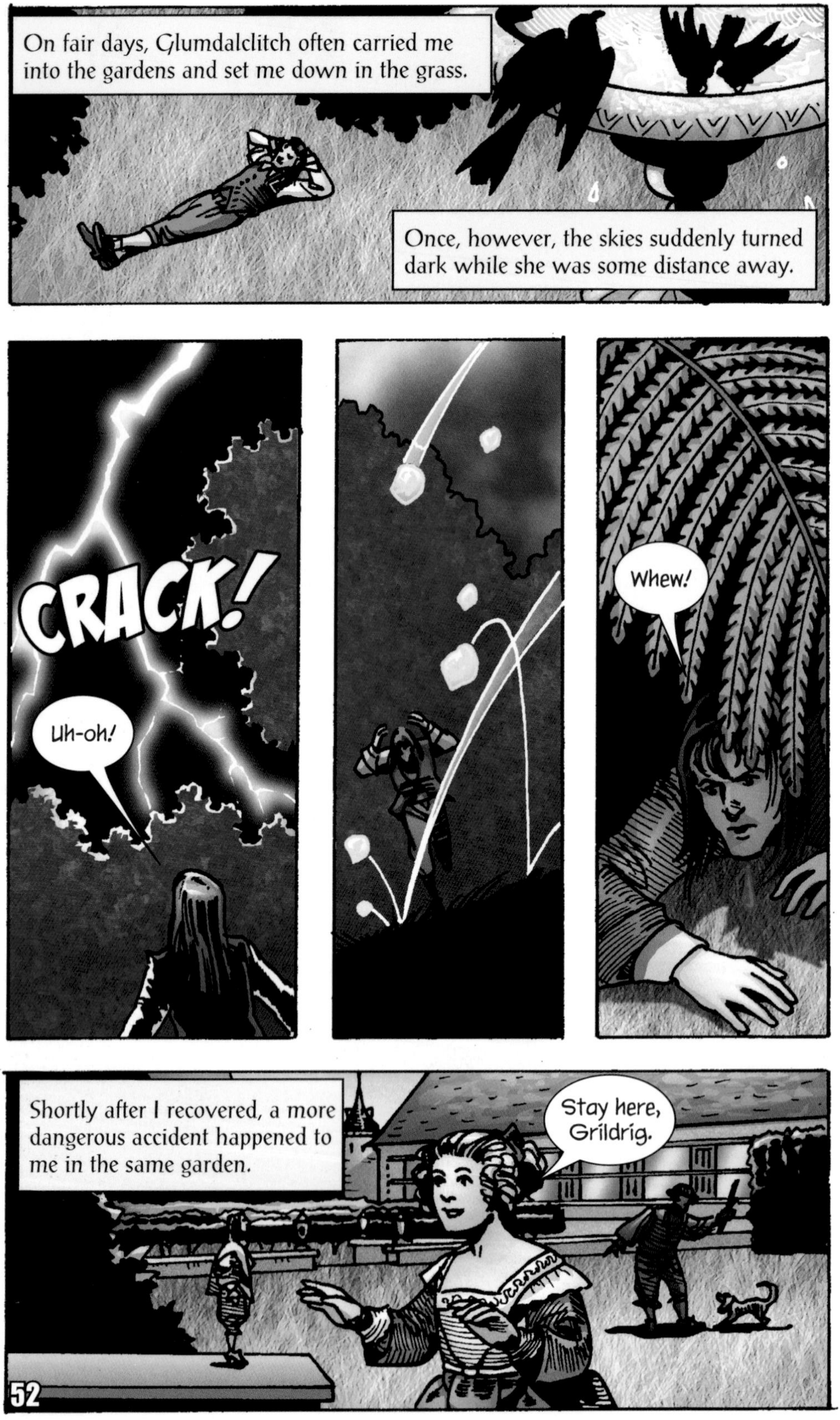
On fair days, Glumdalclitch often carried me into the gardens and set me down in the grass.
Once, however, the skies suddenly turned dark while she was some distance away.
CRACK!
Uh-oh!
Whew!
Shortly after I recovered, a more dangerous accident happened to me in the same garden.
Stay here, Grildrig.

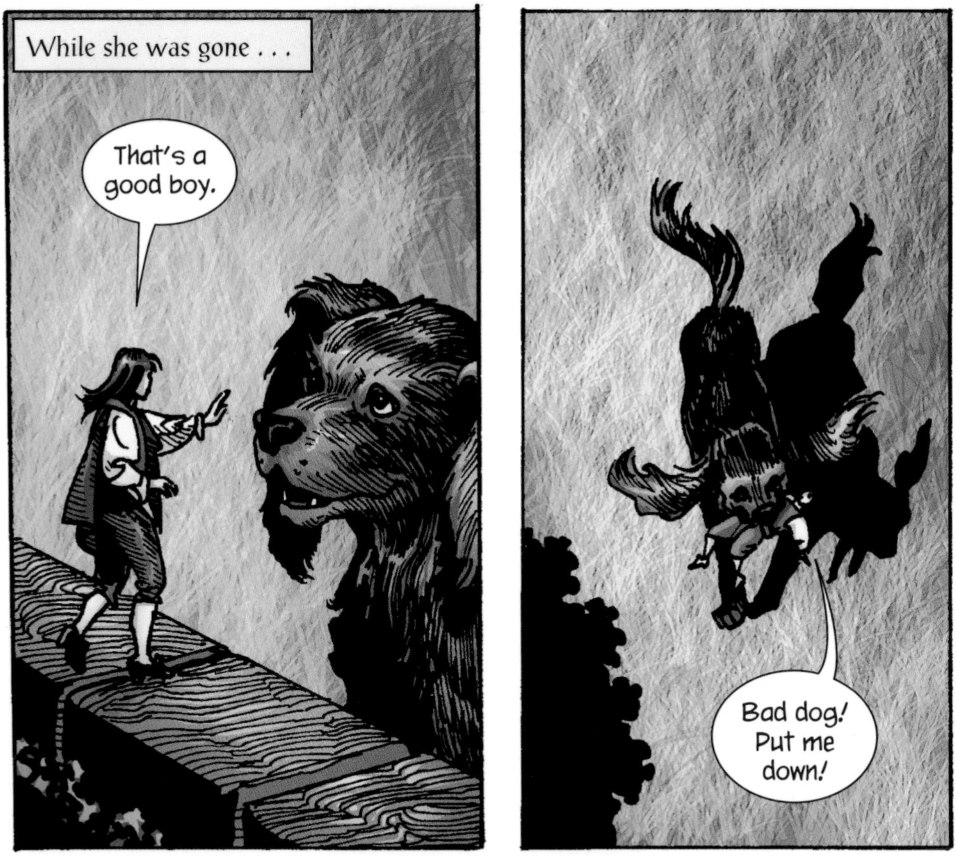
While she was gone . . .
That's a good boy.
Bad dog! Put me down!
Luckily, the dog ran straight to his master.
I'm so sorry.
Grildrig, what happened?!
I'll never let you out of my sight again!

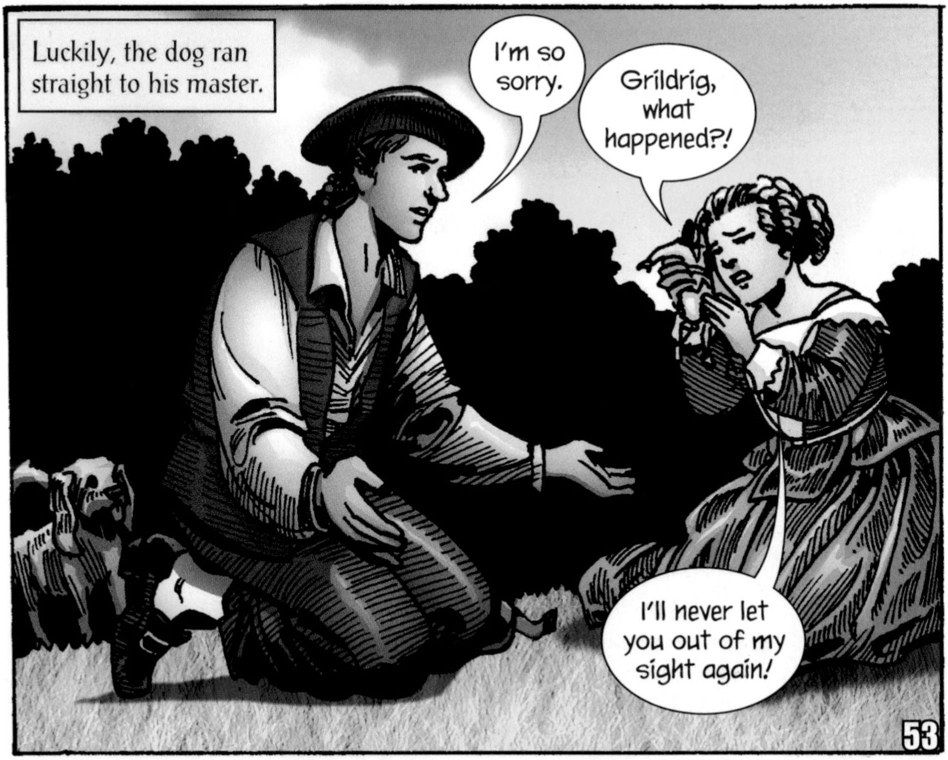

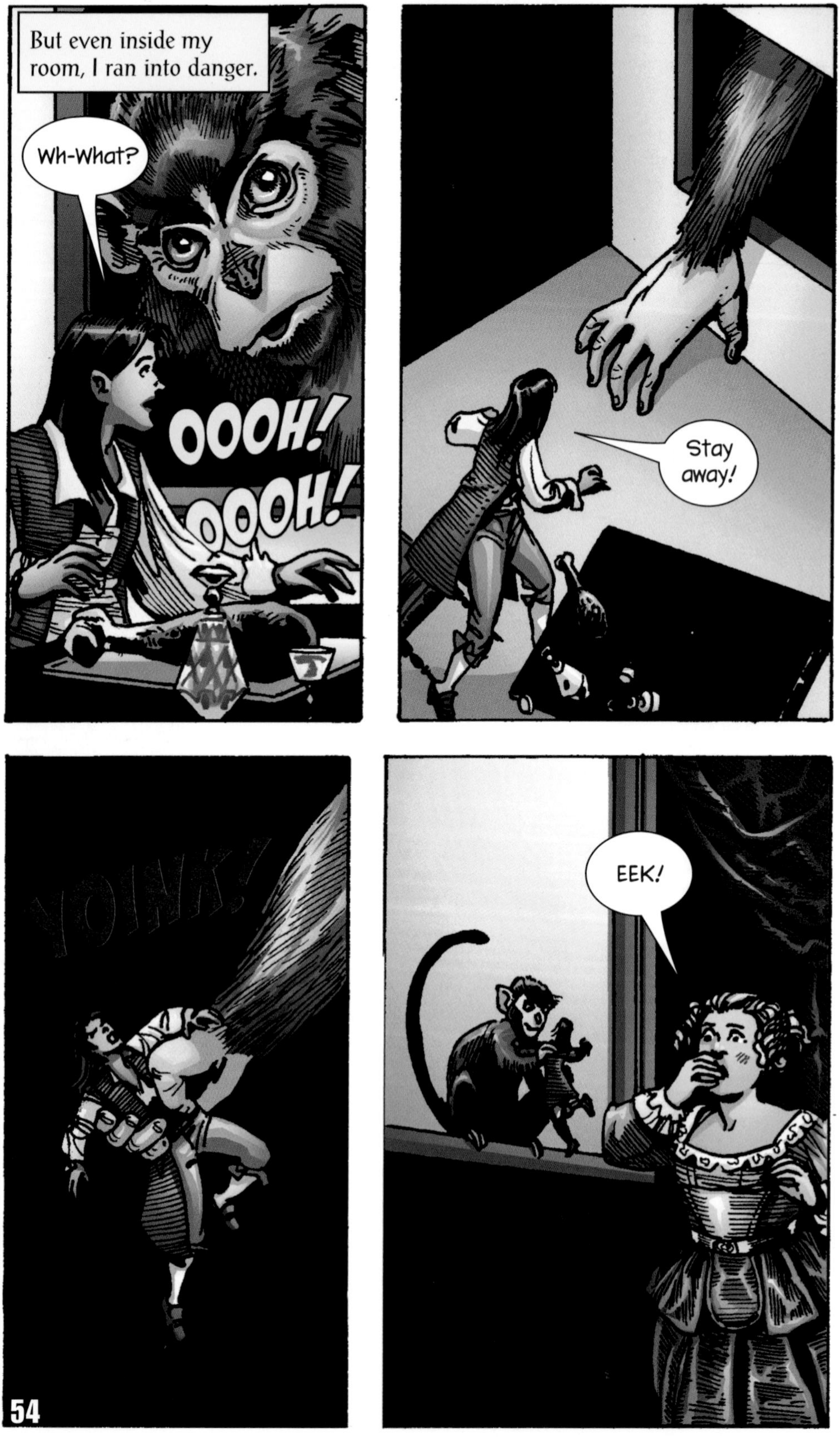
But even inside my room, I ran into danger.
Wh-What?
OOOH! OOOH!
Stay away!
YOINK!
EEK!

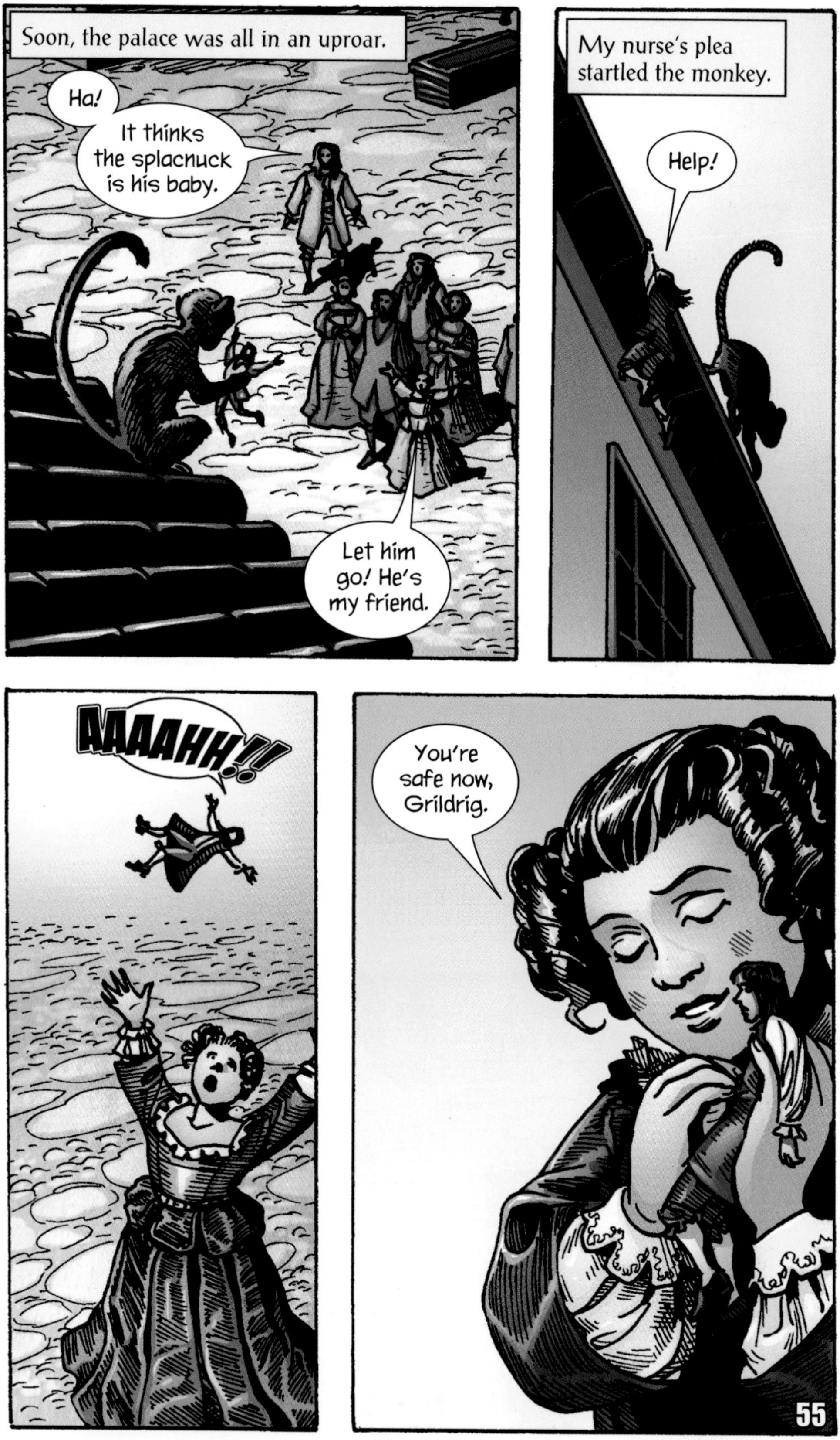

Soon, the palace was all in an uproar.
Ha!
It thinks the splacnuck is his baby.
Let him go! He's my friend.
My nurse's plea startled the monkey.
Help!
AAAAHH!!
You're safe now, Grildrig.

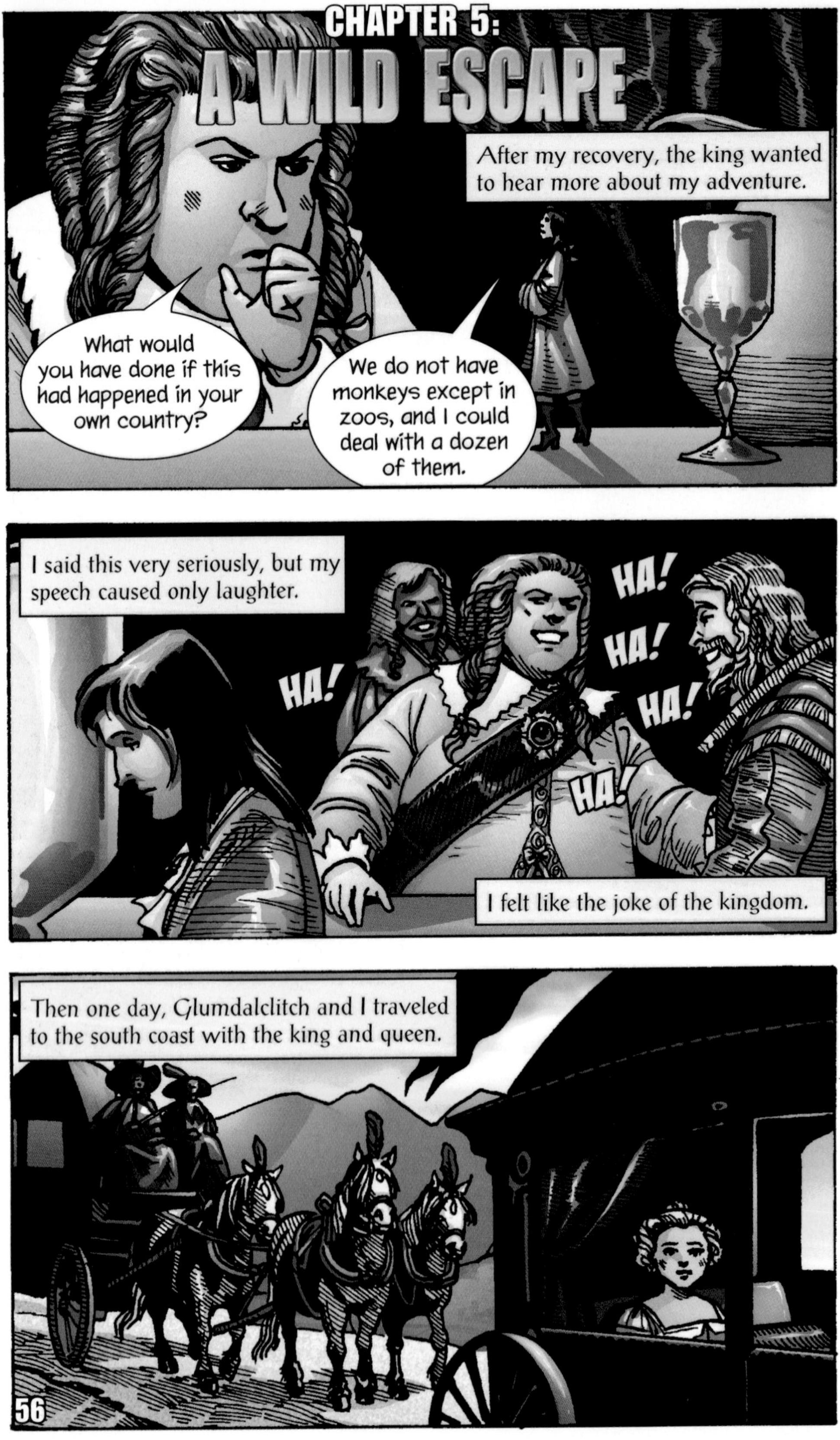
CHAPTER 5:
A WILD ESCAPE
After my recovery, the king wanted to hear more about my adventure.
What would you have done if this had happened in your own country?
We do not have monkeys except in zoos, and I could deal with a dozen of them.
I said this very seriously, but my speech caused only laughter.
HA! HA! HA! HA! HA!
I felt like the joke of the kingdom.
Then one day, Glumdalclitch and I traveled to the south coast with the king and queen.

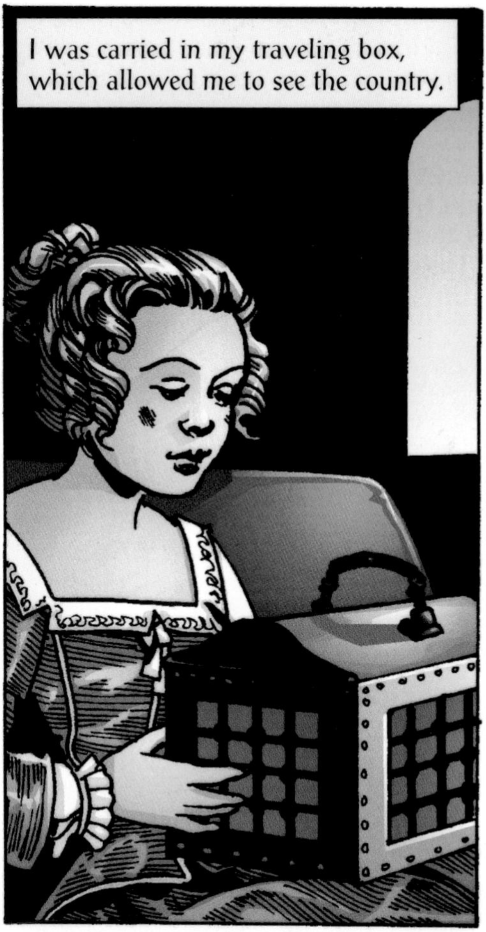
I was carried in my traveling box, which allowed me to see the country.

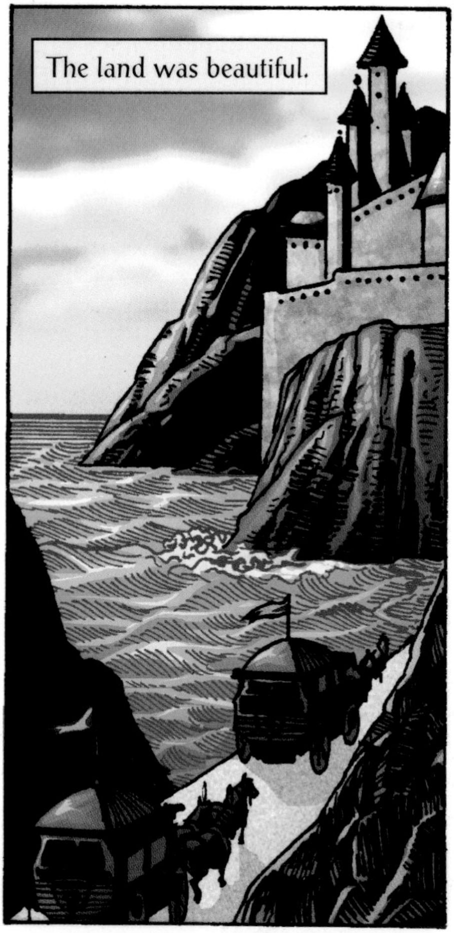
The land was beautiful.

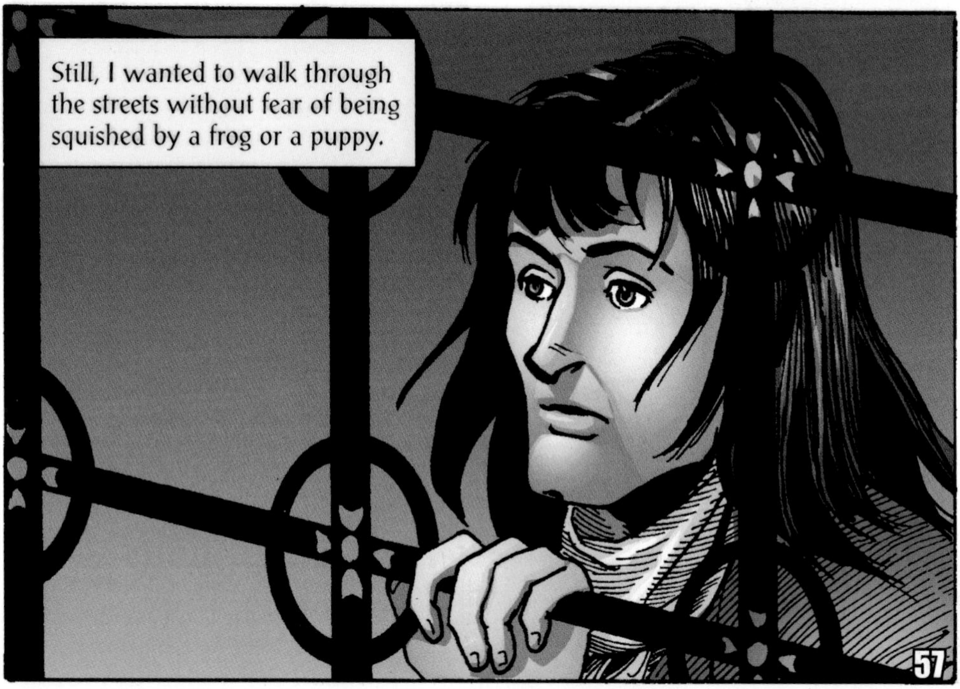
Still, I wanted to walk through the streets without fear of being squished by a frog or a puppy.

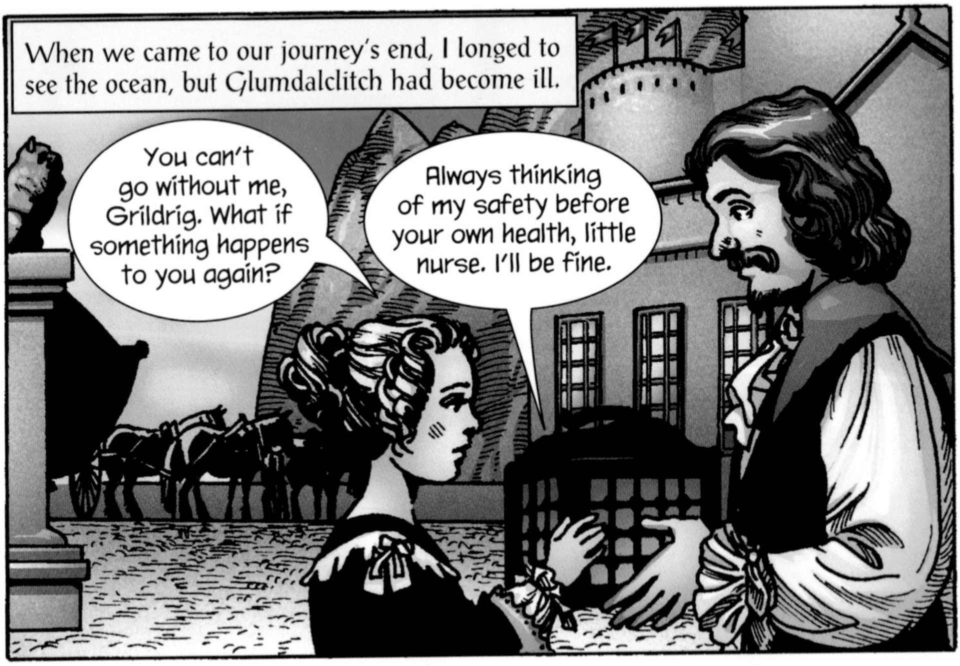
When we came to our journey's end, I longed to see the ocean, but Glumdalclitch had become ill.
You can't go without me, Grildrig. What if something happens to you again?
Always thinking of my safety before your own health, little nurse. I'll be fine.

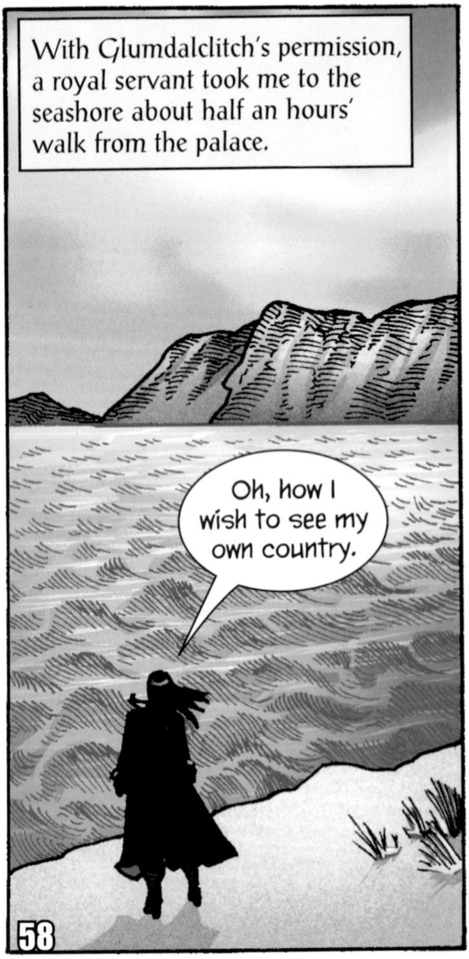
With Glumdalclitch's permission, a royal servant took me to the seashore about half an hours' walk from the palace.
Oh, how I wish to see my own country.

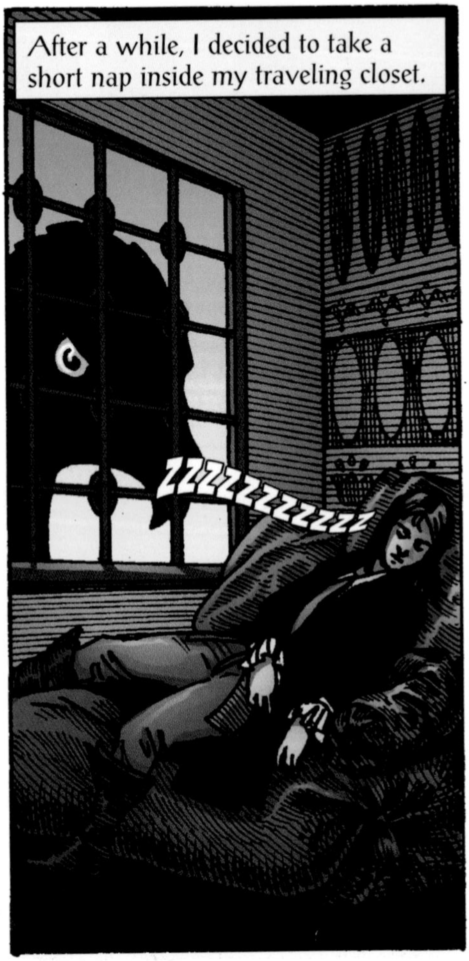
After a while, I decided to take a short nap inside my traveling closet.
ZZZZZZZZZZZZ

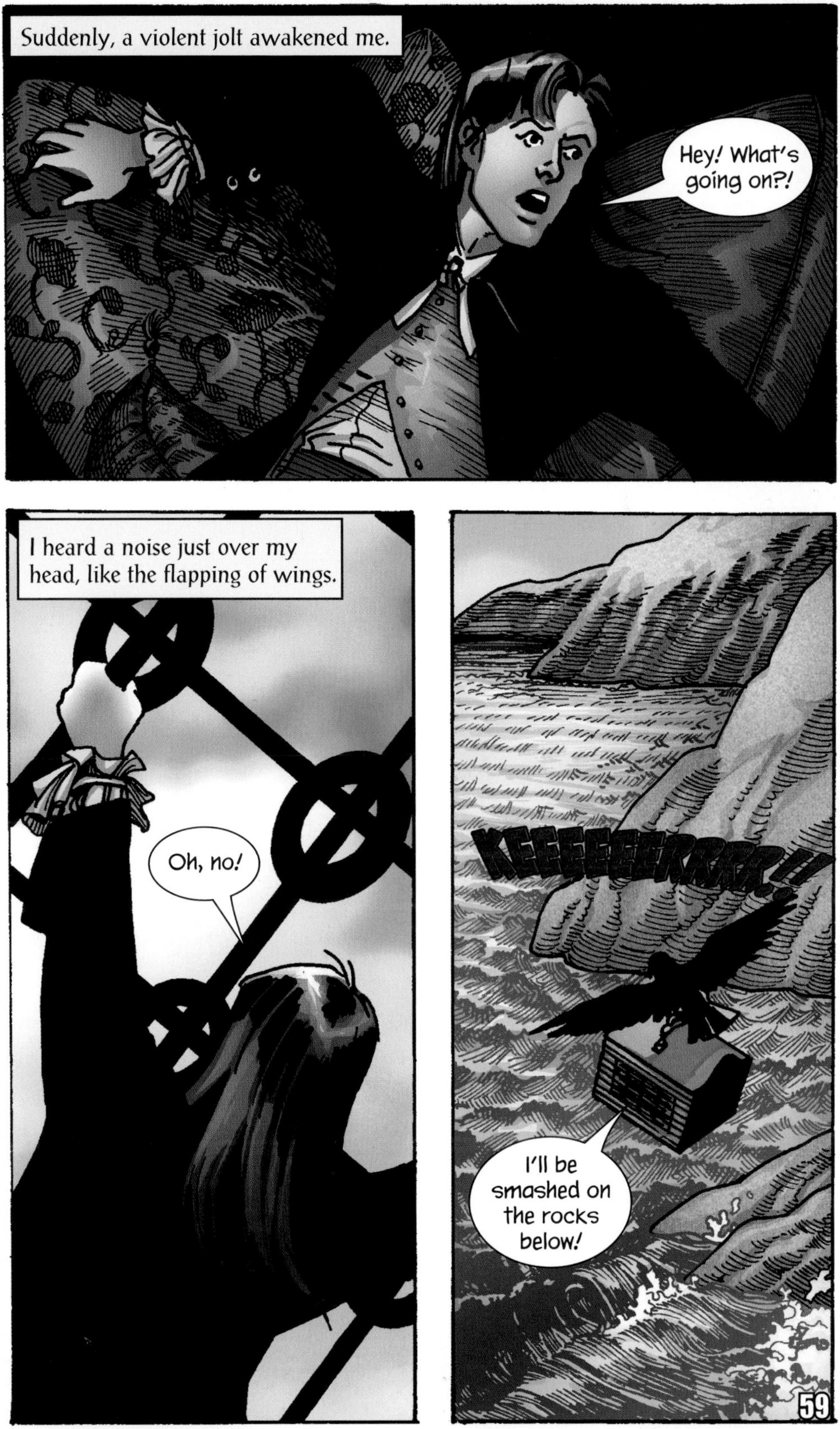
Suddenly, a violent jolt awakened me.
Hey! What's going on?!
I heard a noise just over my head, like the flapping of wings.
Oh, no!
KEEEEERRRR!!!
I'll be smashed on the rocks below!

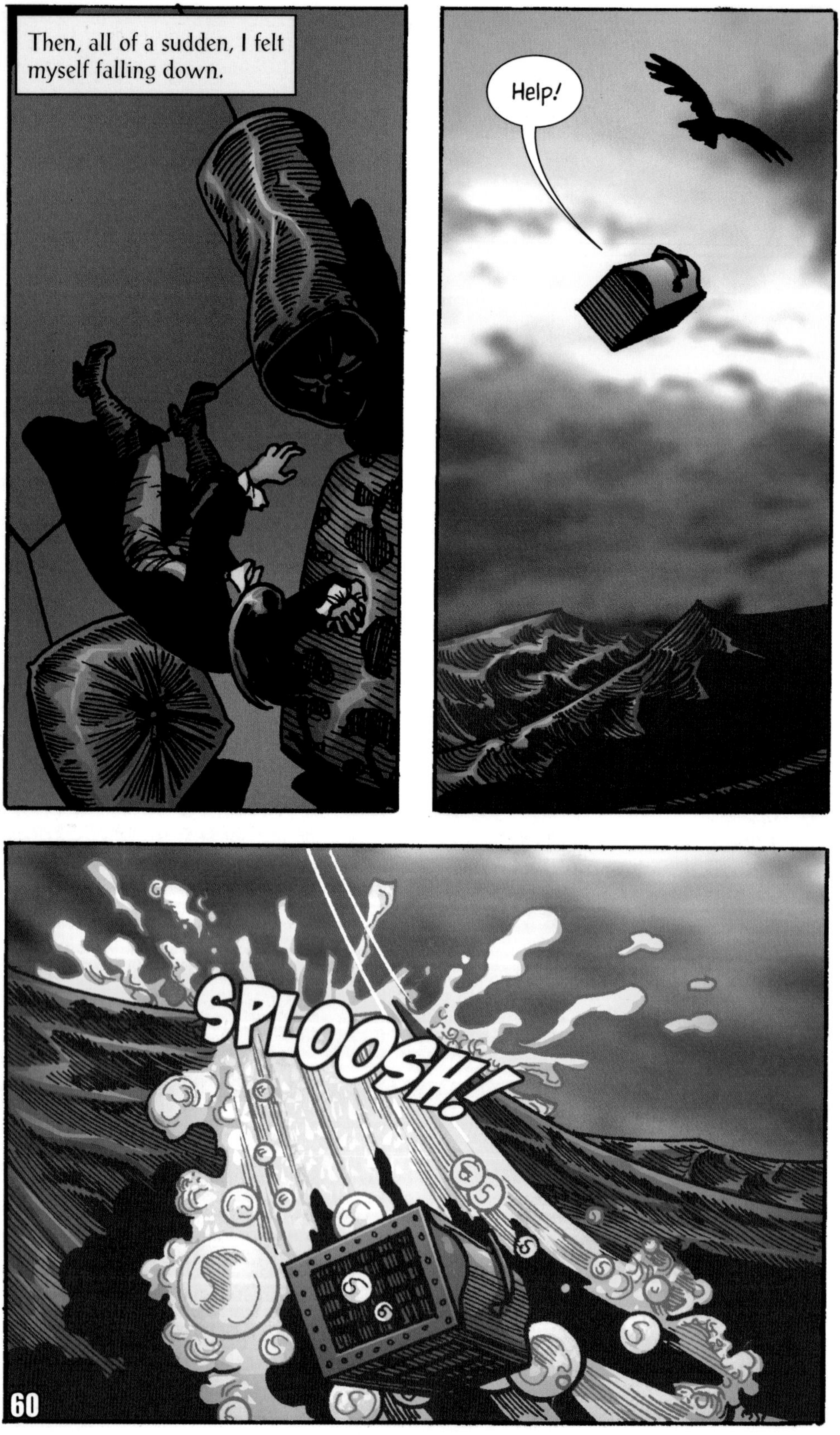
Then, all of a sudden, I felt myself falling down.
Help!
SPLOOSH!

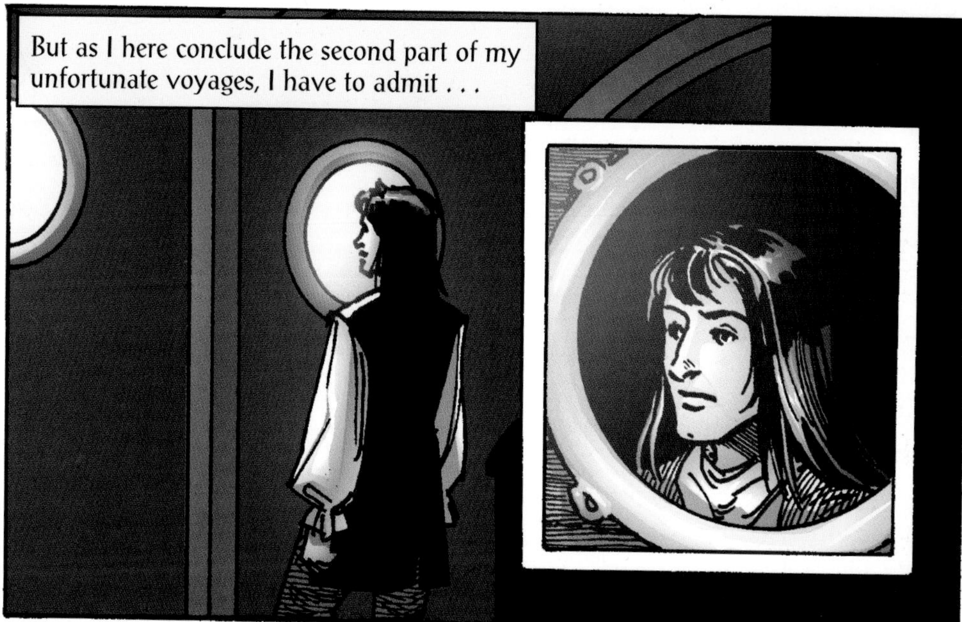
But as I here conclude the second part of my unfortunate voyages, I have to admit . . .

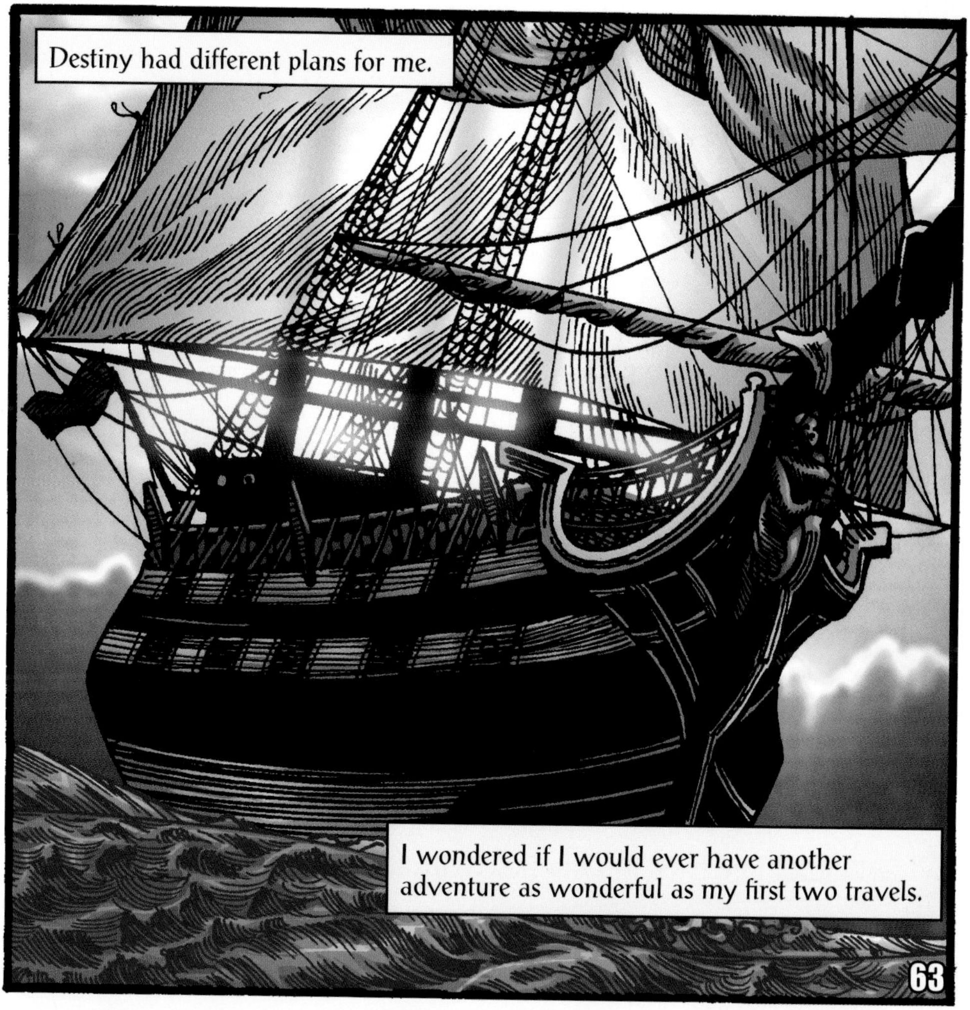
Destiny had different plans for me.
I wondered if I would ever have another adventure as wonderful as my first two travels.

ABOUT THE AUTHOR

Jonathan Swift was born on November 30, 1667, in Dublin, Ireland. His father had died several months earlier, and his mother decided Swift should be raised by relatives. Growing up, Swift enjoyed reading and writing. In 1682, he graduated from Trinity College in Dublin, and then traveled to England with dreams of becoming an important church member. He soon returned to Ireland, however, to continue his education and eventually become the dean of St. Patrick's Cathedral. In the meantime, Swift never lost his love for writing. In 1726, he published *Gulliver's Travels,* a story that is still popular today.

ABOUT THE RETELLING AUTHOR

Growing up in a small Minnesota town, Donald Lemke kept himself busy reading comics, as well as classic novels. Today, Lemke works as a children's book editor and pursues a master's degree in publishing from Hamline University in St. Paul. In his spare time, Lemke has written several graphic novels for kids. This is his first book to combine both his love for comics and classic stories.

ABOUT THE ILLUSTRATOR

Cynthia Martin has worked in comics and animation since 1983. Her credits include *Star Wars, Spiderman,* and *Wonder Woman* for Marvel Comics and DC Comics. Martin's recent projects include an extensive series of graphic novels for Capstone Press and two issues of *Blue Beetle.* She lives in Omaha, Nebraska.

GLOSSARY

capital (KAP-uh-tuhl)—the city where the government is located in a state or country

convict (kuhn-VIKT)—to find proof that someone is guilty of a crime

council (KOUN-suhl)—a group elected to make decisions about a city or country

destiny (DESS-tuh-nee)—the future of your life

emperor (EM-pur-ur)—the male ruler of a country

kingdom (KING-duhm)—an area, usually a country, that has a king and queen as their rulers

liberty (LIB-ur-tee)—freedom from being held prisoner

permission (pur-MISH-uhn)—allowing something to happen

temple (TEM-puhl)—a building used for religious worship

treason (TREE-zuhn)—the crime of going against your own country and helping another country during war

voyage (VOI-ij)—a long journey, often by sea

worships (WUR-shipz)—shows respect to a god

MORE ABOUT GULLIVER'S TRAVELS

At the end of this story, Lemuel Gulliver sails off in search of another adventure. In fact, the original novel by author Jonathan Swift, published in 1726, actually included two more tales of Gulliver's life at sea. Below are summaries of each of these incredible voyages.

The Floating Island

On his third voyage, Gulliver sails aboard the *Hopewell*. Soon, pirates attack the ship, and Gulliver is set adrift at sea. He eventually spots a large object floating in the sky. It is a giant, flying island! The people on the island, called Laputa (lah-POO-tah), rescue Gulliver by pulling him up to their floating country. The Laputans and their king love music and mathematics, and soon Gulliver learns the secret of their floating land. The island hovers above another country by the science of magnetism. During the coming weeks, Gulliver visits the lower land, called Balnibarbi (bal-nuh-BAR-bee), and learns how they dislike the people of Laputa. Gulliver explores other nearby lands, including an island of sorcerers and Luggnagg, where people believe they've discovered the secret of eternal life. Eventually, Gulliver ends his journey in Japan, where he sets sail for home.

The Talking Horses

Gulliver's fourth and final voyage also turns out to be the strangest. While sailing toward the Caribbean Sea, several members of Gulliver's crew turn against him. They leave Gulliver stranded on an island with no way to escape. Soon, however, Gulliver learns that he is not alone. The island is filled with digusting, humanlike creatures called Yahoos. The Yahoos are dirty and gross and begin to attack Gulliver. Fortunately, Gulliver is saved by none other than a talking horse! The horse takes Gulliver back to his house and tells him that there are many other horses like him, called Houyhnhnms (huh-WIN-uhms). The Houyhnhnms rule over the Yahoos, keeping them penned up in cages like pets. Since Gulliver looks like a Yahoo, the Houyhnhnms decide he must live with the smelly creatures or return home. Shortly after, Gulliver builds a canoe and sets sail. But when he returns home to England, Gulliver can no longer stand to be around humans, which remind him of the smelly Yahoos. For the rest of his life, Gulliver spends much of his time in the stables, caring for his horses and avoiding people.

DISCUSSION QUESTIONS

1. On page 39, Gulliver says, "Now I know how the tiny people of Lilliput must have felt." What do you think he meant by this statement? Do you think Gulliver would treat the Lilliputians differently after knowing what it's like to be small? Explain your answers.

2. Gulliver was nearly killed on both of his adventures. Why do you think he still wants to explore and see new things?

3. Would you rather be stuck on an island filled with giants or trapped by an army of teeny, tiny creatures? Explain why you would choose one place more than the other.

WRITING PROMPTS

1. Imagine that you are suddenly shrunk down to the size of a mouse. Write a story about how you would survive a typical day. How would you get to school? What would lunch be like? What challenges would you face?

2. Whenever Gulliver returned to his ship, he wrote down what happened on his adventures so he could share the stories with others. Describe two of the most exciting days in your life. Then, share your stories with friends or family.

3. At the end of the story, Gulliver sails off to explore more places. Pretend you are the author and write your own *Gulliver's Travels* adventure. Where will he go next? What type of people or creatures will he meet?

OTHER BOOKS

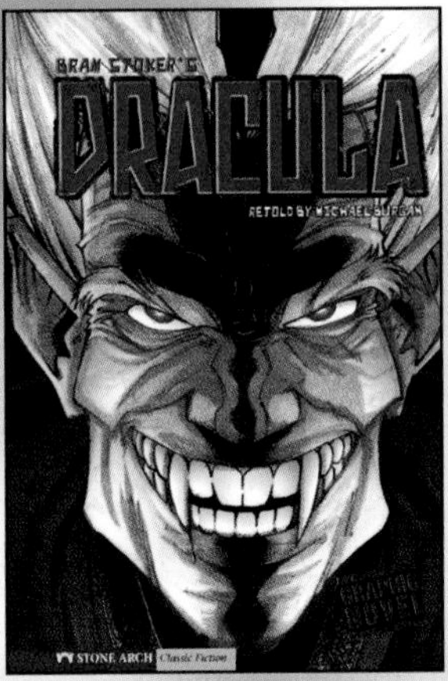
BRAM STOKER'S
DRACULA
STONE ARCH

Dracula

On a business trip to Transylvania, Jonathan Harker stays at an eerie castle owned by a man named Count Dracula. When strange things start to happen, Harker investigates and finds the count sleeping in a coffin! Harker isn't safe, and when the count escapes to London, neither are his friends.

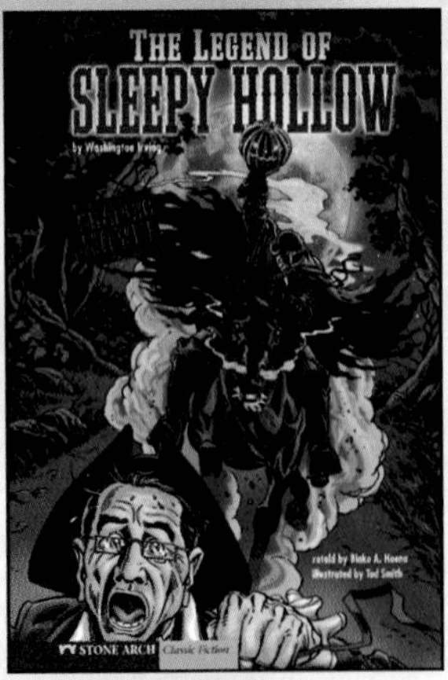
THE LEGEND OF
SLEEPY HOLLOW
STONE ARCH

Sleepy Hollow

A headless horseman haunts Sleepy Hollow! At least that's the legend in the tiny village of Tarrytown. But scary stories won't stop the town's new schoolmaster, Ichabod Crane, from crossing through the Hollow, especially when the beautiful Katrina Balt lives on the other side. Will Ichabod win over his beloved or discover that the legend of Sleepy Hollow is actually true?

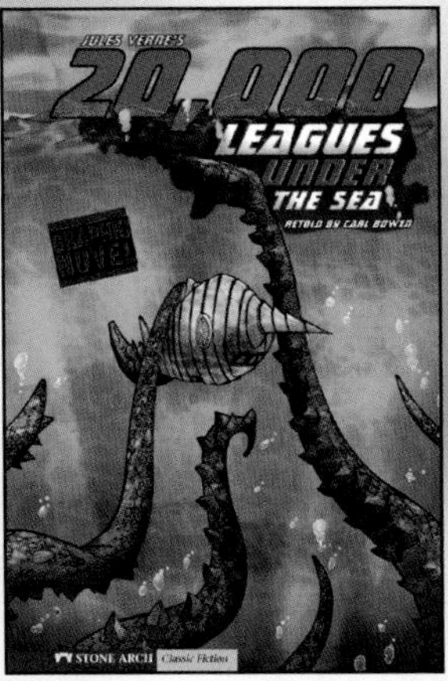
JULES VERNE'S
20,000
LEAGUES
UNDER
THE SEA
STONE ARCH Classic Fiction

20,000 Leagues Under the Sea

Scientist Pierre Aronnax and his trusty servant set sail to hunt a sea monster. With help from Ned Land, the world's greatest harpooner, the men soon discover that the creature is really a high-tech submarine. To keep this secret from being revealed, the sub's leader, Captain Nemo, takes the men hostage. Now, each man must decide whether to trust Nemo or try to escape this underwater world.

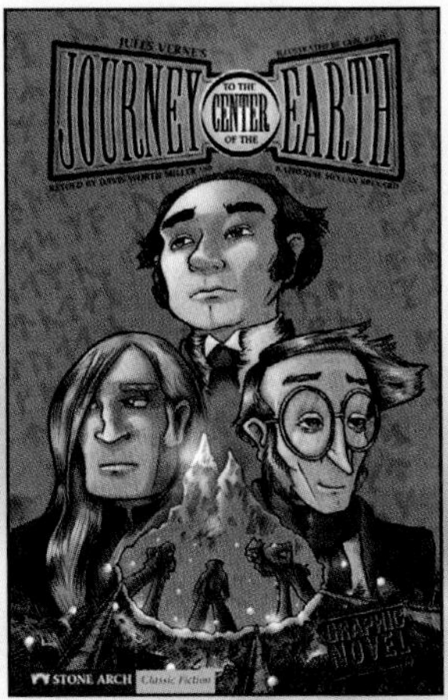
JULES VERNE'S
JOURNEY TO THE CENTER OF THE EARTH
GRAPHIC NOVEL
STONE ARCH Classic Fiction

Journey to the Center of the Earth

Axel Lidenbrock and his uncle find a mysterious message inside a 300-year-old book. The dusty note describes a secret passageway to the center of the earth! Soon they are descending deeper and deeper into the heart of a volcano. With their guide Hans, the men discover underground rivers, oceans, strange rock formations, and prehistoric monsters. They also run into danger, which threatens to trap them below the surface forever.

INTERNET SITES

Do you want to know more about subjects related to this book? Or are you interested in learning about other topics? Then check out FactHound, a fun, easy way to find Internet sites.

Our investigative staff has already sniffed out great sites for you!

Here's how to use FactHound:

1. Visit www.facthound.com

2. Select your grade level.

3. To learn more about subjects related to this book, type in the book's ISBN number: **9781434204493**.

4. Click the **Fetch It** button.

FactHound will fetch the best Internet sites for you!